School

The Seventh Silence

By Craig Herbertson

IMMANION PRESS

Stafford, England

School: The Seventh Silence
By Craig Herbertson
© 2005

Cover: Gabriel Strange/Elizabeth Joan Clarke (photography)
Interior Illustrations: Craig Herbertson
Art Direction and Typesetting by Gabriel Strange
Editor: Storm Constantine
Copy Editor: Wendy Darling

Set Century Schoolbook

First edition by Immanion Press, 2005

0 9 8 7 6 5 4 3 2 1

An Immanion Press Edition
http://www.immanionpress.wox.org
info@immanionpress.wox.org

ISBN 1-9048-5321-8

To 'M'

Whose embassy to the faeries in the abandoned greenhouse procured me a magic potion most efficacious against nightmares.

School

The Seventh Silence

The world is never quiet, even its silence eternally resounds with the same notes, in vibrations which escape our ears. As for those that we perceive, they carry sounds to us, occasionally a chord, never a melody.

- Albert Camus

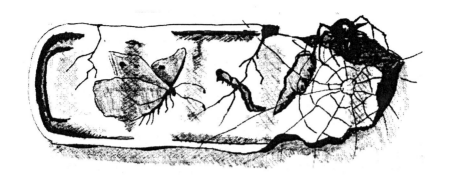

Chapter 1
Papillon

Omnium rerum principia parva sunt.

- Cicero

It must have been the last of the caterpillars: Small, green, flexible and blind, it was searching along the twig for a place to rest. Jean was idling on the back porch. Inside, in the kitchen talking to Auntie May was his little sister.

Jean, thoughtful as ever, was considering the coincidence of finding the caterpillar and Michelle's excited talk. She was playing a butterfly in the drama group at three o'clock after school. It was a chance for Michelle to dress up and show off. Auntie May had spent all the previous evening sewing yellow wings onto a shawl, while Michelle had painted a tight-rolled cardboard body. The colours were all yellow and white.

It was something of a coincidence; Michelle, who had always been nicknamed 'Papillon', dressing as a butterfly, and this sudden discovery of caterpillars in the flowering currant bush. It only needed finding a cocoon

9

and the picture would be complete. The question was, where do caterpillars leave their cocoons? Jean thought it might be under the leaves somewhere and he looked in a dispirited fashion. All that he found was evidence of more caterpillars. They themselves had gone, but the holes left behind were an indication that they had been dining off the bush for some time.

Michelle was so excited, she was talking to Auntie May in a mix of French and English. Jean sighed. Auntie May was Scottish, but had lived in Cheshire for so long that she had entirely lost her Scottish accent, acquiring a flat northern English brogue in its place. She hadn't, however, acquired the ability to speak French. *Somehow*, thought Jean, *she must understand Michelle in the way that women do when they are discussing dressing up. They don't appear to listen but they appear to know.*

The caterpillar reached the underside of a leaf and sat up on its rear legs. It began to project its little button head in all directions like a one armed boxer. There was no way to go except back, but of course it was blind and couldn't know that.

Jean heard Michelle from the kitchen dropping into whole sentences of French. He almost laughed. That was the problem with little *Papillon*. She really didn't know she was in England. At seven, Jean supposed, the world must be a bizarre place. She hadn't even asked questions about Father or Mother. She seemed to be getting along fine.

Avoiding the caterpillar, Jean gently touched the underside of the leaves of the flowering currant. They were a little like the vine leaves in Auxerre, only hairier and smaller. Did they have praying manti here? They didn't appear to have many big insects in England.

He finally found a cocoon. It was resting under one of the lower branches of the bush. He had to bend down and lie on his back to see it. He felt the cold of the back porch seeping upwards into his body and his head felt suddenly fragile, as if might break open like an egg. From underneath, the bush looked strangely different. It hadn't been friendly before – it had just been a bush – but now it appeared almost unfriendly. Jean had a glimpse of how an insect might see it.

For a few seconds, Jean lay looking at the cocoon and listening to Auntie May warning his sister about strangers. The English appeared obsessed with it. Then his eyes tried to focus on the cocoon he had found, and he had one of those moments where you can't see the thing even though you are still looking at it directly. It seemed to leap at his eye: a hollow-looking cocoon uncannily like an old coffin. His body sucked up the cold and a shiver ran through his bony frame. Little *Papillon* appeared to have been able to dismiss all the thoughts of death, the cold hospital corridors, all the tears and all the goodbyes; now she could happily dance around in a charades costume, like one of Fournier's ball guests. In a while, she might even forget her French as Auntie May had forgotten her own dialect.

Jean wouldn't forget.

Lying there, looking at the ceiling of the sky, Jean felt very small. It was a cold sky. Despite a calendar date that read 'summer', light rain had fallen once this morning already and his whole body rebelled against the idea that this was really summer. It was too cold. The sky was the wrong colour and the flowering currant bush was not a vine.

The cocoon had brought on the shivering fit. It looked so dormant, so dry, like the sarcophagus for a mummy he had seen in Manchester museum on last week's school trip. He could imagine what it contained, a hollow dried out skinny thing that had once been human.

A few spatters of rain fell on his cheek, even though the sun was shining. What kind of country was this? Why had his mother sent him here? He heard little *Papillon* laughing in the kitchen. In a minute, she would be running onto the back porch and encouraging him to 'regarde'.

It was lucky that the rain fell.

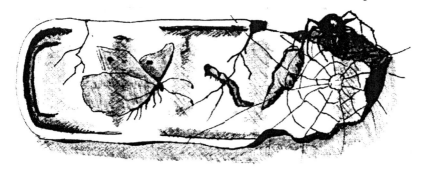

Chapter 2
Morning

I always get the shakes before a drop.
*- **Robert A. Heinlein***

Jean stared at his breakfast. Auntie May had left some Cornflakes in a bowl and a note to say that there was milk in the fridge. There was toast if he wanted it and some juice in the cupboard. She, of course, had left for primary school with his sister. Jean sat alone at the Formica-covered table enjoying the stillness of the empty house.

There was a thing about silence that at once attracted and repelled Jean. He liked to be alone and then the silence was enjoyable. Or at least it would be enjoyable if it weren't for breakfast. For at least three weeks, he had been slowly asphyxiating on Auntie May's artificial juice. At night, sometimes he would dream of black coffee and croissants, but Auntie May was old fashioned and appeared to live in a world composed of packet soups and frozen foods. She didn't even have the equipment to make real coffee. She had scoffed when he had asked about some table wine.

13

Jean sank into the chair. His mother and May were sisters, but even though they looked vaguely similar, they were as alike in temperament as cat and dog.

Jean felt a gagging sensation build from his stomach up to his throat. The thought of the physical similarity between his mother and Auntie May had been too close to the bone. He quickly forced himself to quench the picture of his mother's face before it formed in his head.

The silence was becoming oppressive, almost sinister. It was always the same. One moment peaceful, the next eerie, and now Jean felt as though the cupboards might fly open or the stairs creak to the tread of invisible feet. He got up quickly, leaving his cereal untouched. With his stomach burning, he checked through his school bag again. His hands fumbled through the still unfamiliar books and jotters.

He felt in his pockets for the house key and then threw his jacket over his shoulder. He still found it almost impossible to believe that he had to wear a blazer. When Auntie May had first taken him to the shop, he had thought it a joke. Even though he had read about uniforms in some of his dad's old books, he had really believed that they were part of some fantasy tale. He had considered at that point refusing to wear a uniform, but he knew deep down that any refusal to do what Auntie May wanted would lead to a refusal to walk out of his bedroom door. There was a dark place in his head now, a malignant corner where sadness and chaos lurked. It had appeared from the moment of his departing Auxerre and every action or decision he took had to ensure that it didn't expand to consume everything.

On the back porch, Jean inspected the flowering currant. The cocoon was still hanging under the leaf. By its side, yesterday's caterpillar had already begun weaving its own shroud.

It was time for school.

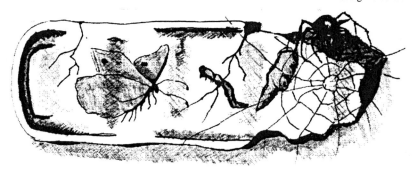

Chapter 3
Personal and Social Education: Part One

'I don't even have a noun for England,' he said, 'just an adjective: 'triste', the sky looks sad, the landscape is sad, the people look sad'
- Pierre

Jean was half French, and even half was a mistake in an English school. Without trying, and with no thought of upsetting anyone, Jean carried himself in a different way. He was from Auxerre, which like his name, no one could pronounce, and he had deep blue eyes with long lashes and he never smiled in public.

He had spent most of Monday morning looking out of the window. If you had been sitting in the back playground, you would have seen his close-cropped hair through the first floor window frame, his slightly too large head, thin neck and pointy shoulders. You would have known instantly that no one particularly liked him.

It was not his appearance as such, although that was obviously *different*. It was not even his silence, which was merely unusual. It was the way he carried himself, the way he moved; a bit like an uncertain spider that

17

thinks it's about to be crushed and should perhaps take things cautiously.

At that moment, however, Jean was neither moving, nor smiling, nor listening to his history lesson. He was staring out of Mr Kent's lower form window on to the windswept playground, thinking about a sequence of bad luck: The kind of luck that would have made the passengers of the Titanic appear like a blessed band of pilgrims on a day trip to Lourdes.

The worst part of the luck had been his name. Why was Jean a girl's name in English? Why had he been called Jean? Where was the sense in that?

Mr Kent strolled down the aisle, fingering his black marker. He was off on one of many long speeches that appeared to have no other purpose than his own entertainment.

'Chimney sweeps: Not many now, but in Victorian times they were a common enough sight. How would you recognise them? Black they were, as black as my cellar. Can you guess why, Matt? Or is listening not on the curriculum?'

It was fortunate that Mr Kent didn't expect or require interruption. Matt, smaller than Jean, but broad like a scrum half, practised a thoughtful look, which appeared to satisfy Mr Kent. He continued his stroll. 'They got black from climbing chimneys. That's how. Nowadays, you have a long set of poles. In those days, you had a small boy, a 'chummy', and merely by the rubbing of his tiny, unfed body against the flue walls you got rid of the soot.' Mr Kent paused and unwittingly joined Jean in an inspection of the playground. 'Not quite as cushy as your paper round, eh, Luke?'

Luke grunted noncommittally in response.

Unperturbed, Mr Kent continued. 'Then one day some fine Englishman introduced Malacca canes and whalebone brushes, which could be pushed and propelled up from the fireplace. That became the universal method.'

'Not universal,' said Jean in a low voice.

'Eh?' said Mr Kent. He was startled because Jean had never spoken to anyone, teacher or pupil, since arriving at Park Grammar. It was a debate whether Jean was more startled than his teacher. He had not intended to speak. Mr Kent joined the rest of the class in staring at Jean.

'In France and Scotland, they used the ball, brush and rope system.' Jean continued, hearing his voice for the first time in an English classroom. It sounded thin and far away, a bizarre, gentle mix of French and Scots. Mr Kent gave an encouraging look. 'The ball was lowered down from the top of the chimney. The weight of the lead or iron ball pulled the brush down.' He was remembering as he went along his father's explanation. Thinking of his father was making it difficult to speak.

'It's one example of the effects of the "auld alliance" between Scotland and France,' he concluded quietly.

Every eye was turned to Jean. He knew that he had just come to that moment which comes to every pupil at school. It was the moment where you do or say something that marks you for the rest of your school career.

So far, he was well aware that no one really liked him. He was French, he was quiet; he was introspective and dull. But then no one really cared about him either. That had suited all parties.

'Yes of course,' said Mr Kent. 'The grand alliance of 1165 against England. Very interesting, Jean. Of course, you have a Scottish mother and a French father as I recall - so, you are something of an international alliance yourself.' Mr Kent smiled. 'But I don't think you could defeat the entire class on your own.'

Jean knew the teacher intended nothing by the remarks except to make him feel at ease. But for the rest of the lesson, Jean felt the less charitable stares of his classmates pinning him to the chair. And when Mr Kent was giving the third warning that morning against 'lifts from strangers', and the class were pushing towards the door, he felt Matt dig him in the ribs. 'Frog,' Matt said simply, but he wasn't smiling.

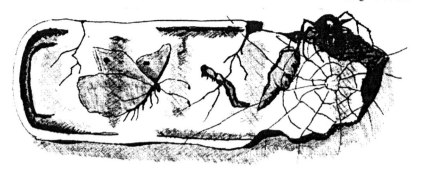

Chapter 4
Personal and Social Education: Part Two

By the last lesson, Geography, Jean knew that his luck, which had been bad, had now plummeted to new appalling depths.

The teacher's voice carried on in a drone. The English were obsessed with a variety of body parts. Jean had noticed that, by a peculiarity of the English language, body parts could be divided into two sections. Section one contained visible bits, which could be talked about in an ordinary monotone, and section two contained private bits that demanded a high silly voice or a low whisper.

Perhaps if he wore glasses they would leave him alone? No. It was the French thing. Why had his stupid father been French? Why could he not have been Welsh or Irish – Russian, American even? He had to be French: Garlic. Frog's legs. Nuclear bombs. French.

And dying in Auxerre, in some stinking hospital, with some stinking, wasting disease that was mentioned in the same tone as the English talked about body parts.

The tears were not far away, but Jean had learned to keep them hidden in his head. There was a sort of waterfall at the back of his eyes, where all the sad bits spilled out, filling his skull with tears. Nobody saw it.

His mother could not, because she was in Auxerre watching Dad waste away and his sister... she was the other part of the problem. Well, not so much part of the problem, but as a spotlight draws attention to a performer, her charm drew attention to his awkwardness and made the problem worse.

Seven years old – why was that a cute age? Why was thirteen the age where they poked you in the back? There was the voice box thing. The hair. The sudden realisation that the entire world, particularly the female half, had discovered that you were ugly and fun to laugh at. But seven: *Papillon* ran about, giggled, gave toys away, invited people to parties, liked Jean, liked everyone. And everyone liked her. She was French. She had the cute accent and the cute nickname. Why was everything cute in *Papillon* and not in Jean?

The rain had started. It rained, and then it stopped, and the sun came blazing out, even as he stared out of the window wishing he were back in Auxerre. English weather in an English summer in an English grammar school. Everything about England appeared erratic and bizarre. But surely nothing could be as bizarre as the game of cricket. What was it? The only resemblance to any game Jean had ever known was the round ball; the *dangerous* round ball that could only be eluded by an almost insane effort of will. (If it ever came near you.) Football. Now that was at least comprehensible: The French had won the World Cup. But then the English had lost it. Even more unfortunately, Jean was no good at it. Another part of this year's sequence of bad luck. English summer, girls, people he knew dying. *Papillon*, as popular as a chart song, and Jean, ugly, inattentive and now unpopular.

The sun sparkled briefly on the staff cars beyond the back playground, lighting up the variety of Morris Minors, old Golfs; cheap cars generally. Except the two

BMW's with personalised plates owned by the office girls. Most English boys thought that the teachers were eccentrics who liked driving cars that would suit a poor country vet. Jean's father had told him otherwise.

'English teachers are not eccentric. They're broke,' he had explained in English. He was trying to help his mother improve Jean's English before he left the green vineyards and the town of Auxerre. Jean's mother was Scottish but he had been brought up in Auxerre in French families, and although English had been spoken at home by his mother, and he was basically fluent in the language, he had never really picked up the accent. In any case, he had never even mentioned his mother's nationality. Mr Kent had spilled the beans in History and had now simply compounded the problem. It seemed that the Scottish struggled a bit on the popularity pole at Park Grammar. Jean sighed and became aware of the silence.

Mr Kay, Geography teacher, he of the sarcastic comments and the teachers' jokes - small, Welsh, obnoxious - was staring at Jean in the middle of one of those teacher silences that means you have been caught.

Someone sniggered. Jean stared back at Mr Kay. More bad luck. If Mr Kay's jokes were anything to go by, he appeared to hate the French more than he hated the English.

'Well, Jean Deforte, you're not interested in saving your own skin then. Perhaps you think you're alone in having a special *protection*, a special *dispensation* from God?'

'Sorry sir.' The safe bet, quickly learned.

'*Frog*,' the whisper came from behind him, but he ignored it and tried to look more attentive.

'You can remain behind, Jean and help me stack some boxes in the storeroom. And Luke...' Mr Kay looked behind Jean. 'You're detained on Monday. Homework club. If there's one thing I cannot stand it's name-calling.'

Something sharp dug in Jean's back as Mr Kay turned to the board.

'You're a dead frog.' The whisper was lower this time and the words were an accurate description of the conclusion of Jean's remaining day. Luke had been born evil. If someone had decided to remake 'The Exorcist', the casting director would be phoning Park Grammar school on the basis of word of mouth. Luke would be playing the devil.

Mr Kay took off his glasses and with them went his obnoxious persona. He appeared suddenly vulnerable, human. A disturbing thought that Jean managed to suppress.

Mr Kay wiped his glasses.

'For once,' he said in his taut Welsh accent, 'this Personal and Social Education lesson has some relevance to you all. I can't emphasise how important it is to be vigilant. You must keep your eyes and ears open. Safety first.' Mr Kay put back the spectacles. Somehow, in the face of it, he was human. He actually cared. Jean shivered. Mr Kay walked over to the window.

'Three kids missing.' He almost said it to himself. 'Three kids from local schools in as many weeks. Look!' He turned around. 'We don't know who or what it is, but you've got to be careful. There could be some kind of monster out there and you could be next on the list. Do not, I repeat, do not talk to strangers, go off in anyone's car, walk home alone...'

The bell rang. For once, there was not the kind of rush to leave that used to precede the National Anthem at Irish cinemas. Jean glanced around. Everyone was pretty sensitive to the sad fact that local kids were disappearing like unlocked cars in Brin.

24

There was a kidnapper in the area, perhaps a killer; someone who stole kids and did horrible things to them. Jean shuddered. Even someone with an imagination the size of a Subbuteo ball would feel a creeping horror when he thought about the butcher's daughter and that little kid in the Echo, whose face had made all the adults tut and look sad, depressed and fragile. What did Auntie May always say? 'If you think you've got problems, think of others starving in Africa.' Or rotting in cellars, or screaming in torture chambers?

Eyes like slow-moving goldfish stared through spectacles at Jean. Not the kidnapper, but for the moment the next worst thing - Mr Kay. He was searching for the ironic quip but stuck at 'Dreaming again, Jean?' The face relaxed into what passed for a half smile. It was not a very good impression of 'cheerful' but it was an attempt. The disturbing feeling that Mr Kay was not really as nasty as he made out came over Jean. Maybe Mr Kay knew about his father. But then he had to spoil it: 'My room directly after form period.'

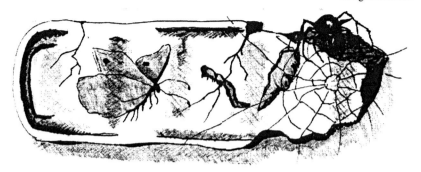

Chapter 5
The Window

*...when the company breaks up: we
shall then see, whether you go out at
the door or the window.*

- David Hume

In the form room, Mark and Matt, the twins who lived
three doors down from Auntie May, sat directly behind
Jean. He felt uncomfortable. He looked across at Luke,
who was grinning in a nasty way, and Jean knew that
the thing he had started in History that morning was
about to really begin. The twins were friends of Luke
and they had never even said 'hello' to Jean, even
though he had seen them on the way to school every
morning for weeks. Mr Kent was talking in the corner
with the girls.

They began by breathing in his ear. He ignored them.

'Chimney sweep.' Said Matt.

He knew there was nothing to do but wait.

'Black, *Froggy* chimney sweep.' Said Mark. Luke was
grinning.

Jean felt something on his neck and he tried to jump
up, but Mark caught him. There was a brief struggle and

Jean managed to pull himself away. Holding his neck. He looked at his hand. It was black, all black. Matt threw the marker pen at him. It bounced off his chest and dropped to the floor. Jean stared at them both. It had begun, as he knew it would.

Luke grinned. 'After school,' he said through his teeth.

'Take those boxes, the red ones,' said Mr Kay handing Jean a key. 'Stick them in the stockroom cupboard, at the back, next to the overhead projector. The old one...'

Jean picked up the boxes. He inwardly cursed his own cowardice. He seemed to remember that he had been brave when he had been Michelle's age. Now he was frightened of everything – drowning, falling, aeroplanes, spiders, embarrassment, silence. The list was endless, but new things like Luke's hatred were being added by the day.

In the cupboard, Jean felt momentarily safe. At least now there was a chance that Luke might not wait for him after school. With his shoulder, he pushed the door shut on its creaking hinges then looked around holding the heavy box: books, a computer, paper, glue-sticks and the old overhead projector at the back. He placed the box on a table and stuck the key in the door.

Mr Kay was talking to himself outside. He was not really that bad. Jean fiddled idly with the overhead projector. He risked a look at some files marked 'confidential', but there was nothing of even remote interest. Turning around, he saw through the stockroom window that the sun had emerged again. The light was brilliant, almost unnatural and it drew Jean to the window as a moth to a candle. It was a big window with cobwebs on three corners and some flies entombed in the top ones. A ventilation grill was on the bottom. Jean leaned on it and examined the little tombs. They were not all flies. In the top right hand corner, a huge spider glowered from its secret passage. It seemed to be staring at the broken remains of a butterfly wrapped in a suffocating cocoon. To Jean it was horribly ironic that the butterfly should have ended up in that cocoon rather than one of its own making. He thought of the flowering currant bush on the back porch. Then, hearing a raised voice, he backed away from the window.

Mr Kay was still talking to himself. No, there was someone else there: The Head of Year? Jean stuck his ear against the door. They'd forgotten about him. And it *was* Miss Kennedy, the Head of his year group. *Why was she here? Everyone knew she detested Mr Kay.*

At least they had forgotten about him. The more Jean delayed the less likely Luke would be hanging around the school gates.

No, they had not forgotten. An atmosphere had descended on everything living; a cold, horrible feeling as though warmth and joy were seeping out of the soles of your feet and leaking onto the floor.

Whispers. Two voices, low and urgent saying one thing in voices deprived of happiness. His sister's name, unmistakable even through the door, bizarre in the flat English accents. He moved closer, placing his ear against the wood. Then he jerked back as though he had been hit.

He could not be mistaken. It was something he had heard too many times in Auxerre: the unmistakeable trembling of an adult voice trying not to break down in tears.

It was Miss Kennedy's voice; not the teacher, simply the woman, whispering in a choking voice the things she had harped on about strangers.

But this time it was not a assembly speech, and in less than a second, she was going to open the door and tell Jean something that he did not want to hear, ever.

Quickly, with shaking fingers, Jean turned the key and locked the door. He took the key out and placed it in his pocket and then he turned into the stuffy brightness of the cupboard. A spear of sunlight dazzled Jean. He felt airy and empty as though the sun were sweeping through his eyes to brush aside the inner shadows. But there, in the corner of his head, a malignant darkness remained like a stain. He fought back tears. After a few moments, there was a knocking on the door.

'Jean, its Mr Kay.'

Jean could imagine Miss Kennedy behind Mr Kay, looking solemn, preparing her words. He buried his head in his arms but that did not seem to shut out the world. Then a low whispering: 'I think he heard...'

He had heard. That was why he was clutching at the window of the stockroom, pulling the shutter free, opening the window, which looked out on to the back playground, a long way down.

'Jean, please open the door. I have to speak to you.'

No, he could not speak to anyone. He could only raise himself up on to the window ledge and gradually pull his body upright, so that he was swaying above the empty playground.

From nowhere, a light rain sieved through the sunlight, swirling about his head and face. A brisk breeze whistled in his ears like a hidden piper. In a couple of seconds, Jean was going to jump off. It was a long way down. His body was going to look like a tomato in school uniform.

They were knocking on the door. Mr Kay was saying something about the spare keys.

The back playground looked close up and far away at the same time. The concrete looked hard. Jean remembered skinning his knee on it when two older boys had ganged up on him for being French.

A door closed in the Geography classroom.

30

'*Pourquoi?*' said Jean. 'Why my sister?' The tears came choking through his mouth and he felt sick. *I'm going to cry*, he thought. *My dad's dying, my mother's away, everyone hates me because I'm foreign and now my sister...* Then in his mind's eye he saw her, dressed as a little butterfly: His sister, his *petite Papillon*, kidnapped by some stranger, frightened, perhaps in pain. Each image struck Jean's stomach like a physical blow. Acid bit at his throat. Tears spilled down his face. He could hardly hear for the roaring of the blood in his head.

Keys rattled in the lock. They were trying different ones. Mr Kay was shouting his name. The wind dropped a little, and the rain stopped again, as though a big hand was catching it above his head.

He was going to have to jump soon. It was the only way to stop the carousel of images, each worse than the last that sped through his brain. Jean felt a charge jolt through his head. It was as though his mind was made of paper and some giant had just torn him in half. The half which dealt with emotions simply blew away with the wind. The other half worked him like a machine, allowing his body to continue breathing his heart to pump, his eyes to see.

In a trance Jean began to look around. The ivy became interesting. The wasps humming in it; the smell of decay. The wind stirring the pale green leaves. His senses were suddenly heightened as though the tears, which had blinded his eyes moments before, now produced a clarifying optical effect. His body began to make motions on its own account. Little by little, Jean inched himself away along the ledge, further from the storeroom window. After a few steps, he heard Mr Kay cursing. A door creaked on old hinges. At the same time his hand reached the window frame of the next classroom.

From inside the classroom the drop to the playground had never looked sickening. A few millimetres of glass were enough to induce a comfortable security. Now, outside on the tiny ledge, the view was like a physical thing. Jean felt the ground itself was willing him to come to her. It was an intimation of why sailors drown as Sirens sing. It was death and beauty all bound up; the terrible attraction of the unknown.

Jean's body kept moving like a puppet. His mind still spun in the air; or at least the half of it that could no longer cope. Then for some reason, Jean became nervous of turning around, because the movement might make him fall off the ledge. This was absurd, because the whole reason for being there was to fall off. In a flash he realised that he no longer wanted to.

With Jean's decision the wind ceased utterly. It was as though he had personally willed it. He heard the voices through the storeroom door; Mr Kay and Miss Kennedy insisting that they needed more help. Miss Kennedy shouting for a caretaker.

Jean poised, tense. Then he thought he heard his name whispered, close, almost behind his ear. The voice was that of his sister. With that little sound Jean's whole being convulsed. The half of his mind which had temporarily departed struck him like a knife in the head. It left a bleeding wound full of painful images. He tried to stop them coming, but it was impossible: His mother crying, his father lying in hospital, *Papillon*... Finally, Jean saw what he had dreaded since his departure from Auxerre: The dark place, the malignant corner of sadness and gloom. The death and decay of all those he loved. His hands opened out in supplication. He opened his mouth to scream.

From behind came a peculiar high-pitched zipping noise like a mosquito in a tent. Jean felt a gust of air, smelt a sweet, sickly aroma. Through a grappling web of ivy he half turned, half fell, backwards through the open window.

He hit his head on the floor and saw, between school desks, the running legs of a child disappear through a slowly shutting door.

'*Papillon*', he said and the world crumpled up like an empty crisp bag.

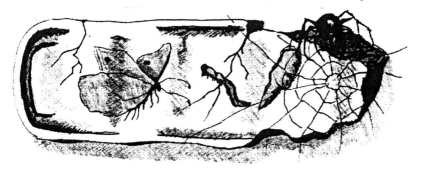

Chapter 6
The Classroom

*Although modesty is natural to man,
it is not natural to children. Modesty
only begins with the knowledge of
evil.*

- Jean Jacques Rousseau

The first thing was the smell: Sweet, sickly, musty; like
old socks, rotten fruit and a whiff of ammonia. Then
there was the taste; a bitter metallic, poisonous sort of
taste, which Jean realised, was blood in his mouth. *Head
injury*, was his first thought, and creeping after that
came 'paralysis', that funny English word, which
sounded like two snakes. Then there was the pain, a cold
numb sensation in his right arm and a beating as
though some little elf was kicking at a door in his head.
His ankle was also hurt, which offered a ray of hope,
because he'd read somewhere that when your back was
broken you could not feel your legs.

For a while, Jean lay savouring the physical pain,
because it shut out his thoughts. There were too many
despairing images lurking in his mind. He kept his eyes
closed as the pain began slowly to subside. He listened

35

but there was nothing to hear. Then he began to wonder about the peculiar smell and the silence. The smell was nothing like the antiseptic odour of the school. The silence was simply wrong.

Jean's fear about his sister and everything else began to give way to fear about what he might see if he *opened* his eyes. Then the sound of deep, deep silence became even more unbearable than what might be seen.

Without moving a limb, he slowly opened his eyes.

He was lying on a dark floor; bare floorboards deeply dark with a dry sticky feel to them, as though if you lay for long enough you might sink into them. And if you lay for longer, you might finally become one of the floorboards.

He shut his eyes again. The little elf was still tapping on the door in his head. And then he left, fading away. Jean realised that the tapping was the pulse of blood coursing through his temples. His heart appeared to be attempting to break the walls of his arteries, as though the capillaries in his head had become too small for the surge of blood.

He heard a tiny moaning noise, still and small like a frightened child in the dark. Then he realised that it *was* a frightened child in the dark. It was his own voice, Jean's, groaning in the blackness.

He opened his eyes again. Floorboards; the legs of chairs – old chairs, old legs, all made of dark wood, all stilled – like a silent, petrified forest.

Somehow, for the first time, Jean realised that this was not a room in Park Grammar school. There was something in the air, something heavy and different; it was that feeling he had had when he had stepped off the plane in Manchester from Auxerre. It was not familiar, known; it was somewhere else. Somewhere that beat to a different drum.

After contemplating this, Jean sat up slowly and examined the bits that hurt. The strange room was not fading with the pains in his body. Instead it appeared to get more real, more intense.

Jean discovered that he was basically okay. His legs had been designed to be skinned and he had had enough jolts, pushes and punches in the neck to survive a few more falls. He stood up. There was an incredible silence, and there were only two ways for him to go; either through the big door or back through the window.

But the window was shut. Someone must have shut it and also, as he walked forward, he realised that they had allowed ivy to grow all over the glass; so much so that it was almost impossible for light to creep in. That explained the new darkness. As Jean peered through the window he could see a quadrangle below. It looked like but unlike the back playground, which was puzzling.

The place was so silent; it was like after-school hours, when all the children, the teachers and the kitchen staff had gone home. 'Outside' looked somehow fragile and unreachable; the dark ivy like some artificial ivy on the cage of an aviary, shutting 'outside' out.

Jean tried the window frame. It was old and stiff. The dark wood was dry to his touch like something out of an old church, not Park Grammar. Why was it so distinct and peculiar? It might be possible to open it, but what then? And moreover: Who had shut it? Even worse, how long did it take for ivy to grow that thickly? A chill uneasiness crept over Jean; he was almost too scared to turn around.

But the room was still there: The old furniture, the flat desks going up in rows towards a large teacher's desk at the top, and in the shadows what looked like a mirror.

Jean walked around the room, between the desks. A deeper anxiety began to steal over him. At first he could not place it. There was something about the surface of the desks that was needling away at him. He had reached the last desk at the top when it fully struck him: No graffiti!

What kind of teacher taught in a room with no graffiti? Appalling pictures rose in his mind, pictures of a sinister sort of demi-god cum devil. A teacher so intrinsically nasty that his students were afraid to write on the desks, even when he was absent. Jean examined the desk again in disbelief. No, there was nothing, not a scribble. Only row after row of dark but ungraffitied desks.

Jean opened one of them: Nothing inside. Then, in a panic, he checked each desk; quietly at first, but then after a bit, not caring about the noise.

Each opened lid revealed the same stark, bare interior. Jean went from the top of the room to the bottom, and then back again. He found nothing: Not a pencil, not an old rubber or a compass or an apple core. On his second attempt, he even checked the underside of the desks, looking for bubble-gum. What kind of school had no bubble gum under the desks?

Jean reached the teacher's desk. It was at this point that he risked his first glance at the ceiling. It was dark under the eaves of the roof and the old globular lampshade looked like a distant moon. He felt the goose pimples on his arms raise. A closer inspection had revealed the impossible.

Not a single paper-and-spitbomb sticky on the ceiling; no star pattern of childhood rebellion, no flicked gobbet of papier-mâché to make a starlit universe of the roof.

Jean sat on the teacher's desk in stupefaction and then, in that moment where you search for the incredible and it says 'hello', he felt the eyes on his back.

38

With a shudder Jean turned. It was as though he were sliding backward down a snowy cobblestone slope leading to a busy main road.

There was no mirror behind the teacher's desk. What Jean had taken to be a mirror was a full-length portrait. It was also the explanation for everything.

This was the Head's classroom. The Head of the school, and he was not the kind of Head you would want to flick a knotted packet of crisps at.

The portrait was full-length, done in oils, a long time ago. The Head had a mortarboard and a gown, and his right leg, dressed in chequered trousers poked out, bending slightly at the knee. His right hand held a cane: It was obviously not for resting on or hill walking, but for hitting people with. Then there was the face. It was really the first thing that you saw, but the whole length of the Head hit you at the same time, giving the face the right kind of nasty setting. In the face, which was pale, with a narrow nose, a pair of black eyes gleamed. They reminded Jean of his mother's old joke: 'The classroom was full of eyes, all the Headmaster's.'

It was one of those portraits where the eyes will follow you around the room

For some time, Jean studied the portrait. It made him feel very small. Jean was frightened of a lot of things, but he was half French, and now he heard his father's voice whispering in his mind. 'If you are ever in prison first check your pockets for the key.' Somehow these words, drawn from some half forgotten memory, comforted him. He tore his gaze from the face and looked at the rest of the picture.

As he did, his hand found something. With a start, he looked down. On the desk was a piece of white chalk. His hand had touched it. He looked again at the picture. In the background were wooden crosses on a low grey landscape that rose up in dwindling perspective. At first, he thought the landscape was a hill, and the hill was Mount Calvary; it seemed obvious, the symbolism would be clear to anyone. But then, as he looked deeper, he realised that that was what you were meant to think. Really, the landscape was flat and only appeared to roll upwards. The crosses were gravestones. The landscape was a cemetery and they were gravestones. The whole picture contained a sense of authority gone mad, like many of the surrealist paintings his father had scoffed at on their last trip to Paris. Jean decided he just did not like it.

The only writing on it was just above the mortarboard. On a brass plaque were engraved the words:

'Head Master'

That was the last straw! The school was wrong, the picture was wrong and Jean did not like it at all. He pushed himself over the surface of the desk and sat in the big leather-backed chair. It swivelled around and he faced the portrait. Somehow, the chalk had crept into his hand and his hand was taking on a life of its own.

When he walked back down the steps to the centre of the classroom, he surveyed the portrait again. Someone, it would always be 'someone' in a classroom, had written just under 'Head Master'

'Are you?'

Jean smiled. He put the chalk in his pocket and then froze. There was something outside the door: The shadow of feet running but no sound.

'*Papillon?*' he said and ran quickly to the door.

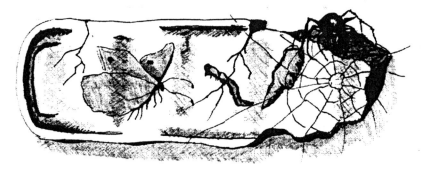

Chapter 7
The Corridor

'*Papillon?*' he said. It sounded like her and somehow *felt* like her. But was it *Papillon*?

The door shut behind him, closing as though it had never opened.

Before him, the corridor stretched in either direction as far as his eyes could see. The floor was covered in a deep red carpet that ran along its centre in a clean unbroken line, leaving thin strips of antique but highly polished parquet on either side. The wood shone even in the dim light, which came from some old fashioned candelabras that were fixed above a series of doors set at intervals along either side of the corridor. They more or less emerged from the shadows in between, like gaps in large teeth. Jean felt that you might disappear into this 'in-between', like a voyager slipping into mud as he traversed a marsh.

There was no sign of *Papillon,* if it had been she. The shadow had disappeared and the only remaining thing was the empty corridor. Jean felt a sick lurching in his stomach. Maybe he had just seen what he had wished for. Maybe she was already dead and this was some kind of ghost world into which they had both fallen. He clenched his spidery hands. He turned around and tried the door behind him. Somehow he knew that it would be locked and it was. There was no going back.

For a long time Jean stood still, assessing which direction to take. Eventually, he decided to go left and stick to that, come what may, because you never know where you might end up, gallivanting around aimlessly.

The doors looked huge, almost unnaturally big, as though the school were intended for giants. It reminded Jean of his impression of the first day at his English Grammar school. Everything had looked entirely too big then and he had felt entirely too small. After a bit, of course, it got to be the opposite way around.

As Jean walked along, his feet sinking slightly in the red carpet, he noticed that after every classroom door there was a square alcove in the wall, like a recessed cupboard with the door removed. It looked as though at some point in the past radiators had occupied the alcoves. At some later point they had been taken away - which had been a bad idea because the corridors were freezing cold and Jean only wore his thin school uniform.

After a bit, he practised jumping into each alcove as he passed the doors. He was just big enough to fit inside with his spidery legs bent a little. This was a pointless game; like running a stick along a rail to see what noise it would make, and Jean felt slightly too old for it, but he did it all the same, because he was alone and you have to do something extremely stupid to be stupid on your own.

'Psst. Have you any buns?'

Jean jumped again but this time it was involuntary.

'Hello?' he said, trying to make talking to thin air sound plausible.

'What's 'ell', pudding or savouries?' said the voice.

'It's neither,' said Jean, scratching his head.

'Never heard of that, but just pass it here if you would be so kind.'

'Where?' said Jean? 'But it isn't buns.'

'Here,' said the voice, 'but what isn't buns?'

'Where?' asked Jean. 'Neither' and 'hello',' he added, beginning to make some kind of sense of things.

'Well, why tempt me, you scoundrel?' There was a half laugh.

"Scoundrel'? What kind of word is that,' replied Jean, thinking "I'm not English, but if I was I'd want to put that word away in a cupboard for a bit."

'It refers to vagabonds, scurrilous cheapskates, cheaters and damn-your-eyes lag faces,' said the voice dryly.

'Well, I'm none of these things,' replied Jean, gathering strength. 'I'm from Auxerre.'

'Ah, that explains it...'

'Where are you?' said Jean. 'In the air?'

'Auxerre,' said the voice meditatively. 'Oh, down here, I should have said.'

Jean turned and there behind him on the floor of the alcove was a grille. In the far corners of the right and left hand of the grille were four fingers and the tips of two thumbs.

Jean bent down. 'Ah, there you are,' he said. 'I didn't know where your voice was coming from before.'

'Me neither, but you're not from here, you're from Auxerre and that explains everything,' said the voice.

Jean still could not see the face of the person, if that's what it was, only the fingers holding the grill from underneath.

'I don't seem to understand the things you say, really,' said Jean.

'Me neither sometimes,' said the voice sadly. 'Don't you have anything to eat, then?'

'I don't think so.' Jean began rifling through his pockets in a hopeless way.

'No cream buns?'

'No'.

'Not one?'

'No'.

'Well, I can't hang around here much longer.'

'Wait,' said Jean. He did not want to lose his only contact in this place.

'I told you I can't,' said the voice. 'You know, only someone from Auxerre would take the kind of risks you take. Well, only someone from Auxerre or an out and out balloon-backed madman.'

'What's a 'balloon-backed madman'?'

'An out and out lunatic, spare, nutcase, *dummkopf* and go as you like,' explained the voice. 'I'm afraid I can't hang around.'

'But tell me. What's the problem with 'out here'...?'

'You must know. Can't you feel it?' said the voice. 'If you make it, see you in Science. Be lucky.'

'What's your name?' shouted Jean and then quickly, 'Have you seen my sister?' But suddenly the hands slipped from the grille and Jean heard an 'aaah!' slowly disappearing like the siren of an ambulance on its way to some accident at the other end of town.

It seemed that the voice had said 'Auxerre' quietly before the hands disappeared but Jean could not be sure.

The corridor was so silent after the voice had faded that Jean felt quite uncomfortable. He discovered then that there were two types of silence. The first was the deep and still silence that he had initially encountered in the corridor and the second was the silence that had followed the voice. The voice, despite its mocking words, appeared friendly and when it had disappeared, the corridor became deep and still and empty. The red carpet appeared to be literally eating up all the sounds, even those of his own breathing. The little candelabras flickered like hesitant ghosts, debating whether to enter or leave the world.

Jean shook himself. 'Science,' he said to himself. 'I suppose it's a direction of sorts. It must be a room, I suppose. And what did the voice mean by saying that I must be a ... 'balloon backed madman'. There's nothing here but quiet and...'

Jean hesitated like the lamps. Quiet and... something creepy, large and coming down the corridor. He could not see it. He could not hear, smell or taste it, but there was a type of ambience in the air. It was a quality of the spaces between molecules, that was rushing invisibly, inexorably and insanely towards him, almost as though it were coming from inside himself, as though he were a computer and someone remote had just switched him on.

Without any hesitation, Jean ran. He sensed which way *it* was coming and he did not want to be there when it arrived.

But he was too slow. A vague mist, not really seen by the eyes, was rising from the carpet. It looked as though it was thinking of coiling around his feet.

Without another thought, he pushed himself against the nearest door. It was big. It was heavy. But finally it was open.

He almost fell into the classroom. A voice spoke in a loud and snappy way.

'Come here. Come here with immediate effect!'

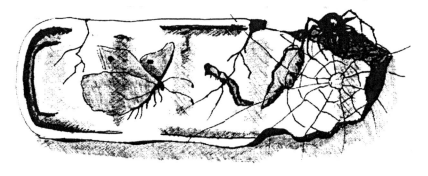

Chapter 8
Chemistry

Logic: *The art of thinking and reasoning in strict accordance with the limitations and incapacities of the human misunderstanding.*

- Ambrose Bierce

For a second Jean was completely blinded by light. It was as though he had been a fish swimming in an underground river and the river had thrown him out on to a beach in the blazing sun. As his eyes became accustomed to the light, the voice shouted again.

'I said 'with immediate effect'!'

Jean, wise in the ways of schools of various types, made his way towards the direction of the voice, even though for a few moments he could not make out anything. He found himself in front of a desk, behind which appeared the tiniest head he had ever seen, rising from the white curtains of a coat and wearing massive black spectacles. For a few seconds, he simply stared at the tiny head in disbelief and then a voice that was too big for the head shouted: 'Why are you early?'

'It was a mistake,' replied Jean quickly.

47

'Oh yes, a mistake.' A huge hand gripped the spectacles and made to clean them with an equally big kerchief. 'If you are ever early again I will send you to...' and here there was a pause, '...the Games room.'

This did not seem like much of a punishment but Jean tried to look suitably impressed. By now, his eyes had become accustomed to the light. He saw that the desk was covered in beakers, containers, cruets, tripods, test tubes, retorts, stands, mirrors, bubbling liquid and gleaming glass. And as the man, who Jean judged to be the Chemistry master, stood up, his head seemed to grow immediately.

'Ah, you were behind a magnifying glass,' said Jean triumphantly.

The head, now normal size, blinked for a second with weak and harmless eyes, and regarded him sympathetically. The hand, normal sized, put the glasses back on and the other hand wiped the bald head, then pointed at Jean. Jean looked at the finger and then the bespectacled face. With the speed of a child removing a drawing from a magic board the sympathy had been wiped away.

'The magnifying glass was in front of me and don't you deny it,' said the chemistry Chemistry master, his voice shaking with sudden anger.

'True,' replied Jean. 'But you were also behind it.'

'My boy, you are in deep trouble already for not being on time. Answer these questions quickly without thinking of the consequences.' The master stared at him with wild myopic eyes and then held up his small thin fingers to make each point. 'Firstly, do you agree that I was behind the magnifying glass?'

'Yes.'

'If a thing is in a place, is it in a place?'

'Yes.'

'Am I a thing?'

48

'Well, yes.'

'Was I in a place?'

'Yes.'

'What are the consequences of being in a place?'

'Eh...you occupy...'

'I told you once and I won't tell you again. Do not think of the consequences.'

'Eh?'

'If a thing exists, does it exist?'

'Yes.'

'Does it exist as one or two things?'

'One, if it's a single thing.'

'Am I a single thing?'

'Yes.'

'Can I exist in two places at once?'

'No.'

'Did you agree that I was behind the magnifying glass?'

'Yes.'

'And therefore...' Here, the master slapped his hand on the desk and all the beakers and glassware, the stands and the liquids, clattered like a boy doing his mother's dishes when he wanted to go out. 'And therefore, if a single existing thing can only exist in one place, then I must have been behind the magnifying glass, and it follows that the magnifying glass could not be in front of me because...' Here the Chemistry master stopped and scratched his head. 'It doesn't work,' he said finally.

'Oh,' said Jean. There seemed to be something wrong with the whole train of logic, but he could not quite place it either.

'You see,' said the bespectacled man finally, 'it's not about *where* you are. It's really all a question of *who* you are.' Again the hand grew small as the Chemistry master sank behind the cluttered desk like a dwarf hiding in a hall of mirrors. 'You see now, for you, I'm behind glasses, and for me I'm behind glasses too; two times, twice, that is.' A laugh that appeared to be too low for the distorted head emerged and rattled through the air like a baritone unexpectedly trying to shatter glass by low vibrations. Everything else began to rattle in accompaniment.

'But I'm behind glasses for you too, two times,' replied Jean.

'No, you're in front of glasses and expect nothing less.'

Jean took the laugh as a sign of relaxation in discipline and risked a glance over his shoulder.

The classroom was not tiered as the Head's had been. It was on a single level. There were big benches made of solid oak in ordered rows, and on each was a conglomeration of glassware like little miniature glass castles drawn from some absurd fantasy. There were no other pupils.

'Isn't this Science?' said Jean, after a moment's reflection.

'Certainly not. This is Chemistry,' replied the Chemistry master.

'But that's a science,' said Jean.

'You don't seem to have learned anything here,' said the Chemistry master, his voice appearing to grow smaller. 'Don't you remember that a thing can only be a single thing? It can't be two things at once. You'd better sit down. That might help you concentrate.'

Jean moved slowly to the back of the class, walking between the benches. He noticed that the beakers were bubbling over slowly and giving off steam. It had been this, and the bright confusing lights, that had made it difficult for him to see earlier. Sluggish liquids ran through the glass tubes and the drips. There were low whistling noises everywhere.

Jean sat down at the very back of the class behind one of the glass castles. For a while, he thought about what to do next. Meanwhile he let his eyes play along the beakers. He heard the coughing of the master like a steam train tunnel-hopping, and then he gasped.

In the lowest beaker of the apparatus before him, he saw a tiny man in shining clothes like a knight carrying a pin or some other weapon, struggling against the bright liquid. The little creature was pushing and shoving, trying desperately to get to the next level. He fought like a man trying to swim against rapids. For minutes Jean sat and watched each attempt with fascination. There were tiny things like sparks in the liquid and the little knight was fighting them with the pin.

Eventually, after what seemed ages, the knight beat his way through the sparks and the liquid, and like a salmon breaching rapids flipped over and through into the next beaker, where he floated around desperately. At this point, Jean took in the complexity and the number of levels. The task appeared impossibleHe peered closer. What was the little knight trying to do? It was like following a Chinese puzzle, but finally, after mentally unravelling all the convolutions, (and backtracking too many times to count), his eyes rested on the highest beaker. Here the liquid had entirely evaporated. There was a little hole in the top and yes! There was a similar creature, only about half the size of the knight, but it was not struggling. It was not, in fact, doing anything. The little creature appeared to be entirely dormant and Jean wondered why, as it seemed to be related to the other little fellow, it did not help him. And then in a flash of reasoning he realised that it could not. It was not that it was trapped; it was simply that it would be of no help for it to go back down the tubes.

Absorbed by all this, Jean noticed that the little knight had reached the next level and somehow had shrunk slightly. The little Princess (this was the best term he could think of) at the top of the apparatus appeared to radiate a little joy, and it was then that Jean realised that she *was* doing something. He heard the voice of the Chemistry master low and threatening through the steam. 'Yes. What kind of activity is it that occupies an eternity that can fill it and be it?'

Jean heard slow footsteps approaching.

'I think you may have guessed something, but this is Chemistry, young boy, and in order to learn, you cannot simply observe; you must transmute.'

At this Jean started upwards. 'What?'

'Transmute. Change.'

Jean experienced a sudden intuition of danger as he looked at the Chemistry master, who was emerging through the steam like a dim phantom.

'And to transmute you must *be*. You *are*, are you not? Or are you *not?*'

'I am,' said Jean 'but I don't need to transmute.'

'Oh yes you do. You need to enter the shining glass.'

'I wouldn't fit and I wouldn't want to anyway,' said Jean.

'But this is School, boy, and here we can make you fit.'

'I don't fit,' said Jean. He already knew this; he had the experience of Park Grammar school to help him.

'Not now. You don't fit *now*.' The little man was very close and seemed to have grown. 'But in Chemistry we have the power and the desire to transmute and change, and in this classroom you will change. You *will* fit.'

'You can't change me,' shouted Jean. He had also risen to his feet. The master was walking slowly towards him.

'But you changed as soon as you entered Chemistry.'

'I'm the same,' said Jean, moving in between the

benches,

'Exactly the same?' said the master.

'Exactly.'

'Every single thing about you is different down to the last cell of the fingernail on your little finger.'

'But,' said Jean edging towards the door, 'if I had changed there would be two 'Me's', wouldn't there?'

'Yes,' said the Chemistry master, triumphantly.

'The one who walked in and the one standing here by the door.'

'Yes,' said the master, in a more puzzled tone.

'And if I keep changing, then I can't be really here and you can't really touch me, because I'm not really here.'

'True.'

'And now I'm completely gone, because...'

He shut the door behind him.

'...I've walked out into the corridor.'

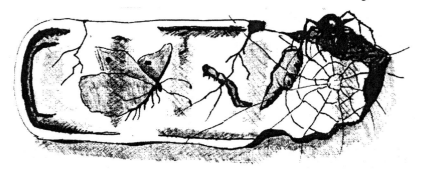

Chapter 9
The Applause Box

Hell is a half-filled auditorium.
- Robert Frost

The corridor was the same, but not quite. The red carpet, the doors, the lights, the pools of darkness; they were all the same, but the air had been...moved. Almost like a forest after a storm. Everything had changed with this release, and the feeling of pressure that had existed before was completely gone.

'Thank God for that,' said Jean, but his voice seemed too loud. He walked quickly but carefully along the corridor, searching equally quickly with his eyes for signs above the doors. As he walked, he briefly sensed that the thing in the corridor was somehow returning. It was like the pause before a breath; not really anything, but it had to come, or there would not be a breath. He quickened his pace, but like a fly buzzing trapped in a cobweb, he felt that the more rapid his movements, the faster the response of the thing.

For a second, he hesitated. There was a recess in the hall and a draught of musty air was hanging around it.

He felt at once frightened but also for some unaccountable reason exhilarated.

In the darkness of the eaves, so large that he had assumed it was some deformation of the wall itself, was an immense picture. For some equally unaccountable reason, the picture scared him senseless.

It was of boys playing some game: Something like rugby or handball. One boy was at the forefront, all face and hair, and the others appeared to be running behind him. At first he thought that the boy was being supported by the others, that he was the leader, perhaps carrying a ball or directing a charge against the opposing side.

But then as he became accustomed to the light he saw the boy's eyes. He knew in that instant that the boy was not leading the other boys.

He was being chased.

The chill began to tickle his legs, like the goose pimples rising on his neck and back. The musty reek had become a tangible thing. He backed away from the picture in terrible indecision. The indecision resolved itself into desperation. Quickly he paced up the corridor.

Almost immediately, he came across an open door. Above the door was writing in a language he could not understand, but there were two masks on either side of the lintel that he did recognise but could not quite place. One was laughing and the other was crying. Both appeared empty, as though no face had ever been placed behind them. Jean stood at the threshold of the door. The space beyond was in pitch darkness, so he hesitated, and then felt the upsurge of fear starting in his belly. The thing in the corridor was coming, whatever it was, and so he quickly, quietly stepped in the dark room and shut the door behind him. He stumbled forward into the darkness, hit his knees on something, fell over and then slowly pulled himself up.

There was a moment of deathly silence, and then slowly, like a giant sea monster rising from an immeasurable depth, deep music began to play; a long, solemn seemingly unending chord that rose in volume until it was deafening.

Jean held his ears, thinking that they might burst but he kept his eyes open, in case something might happen. As he clutched his aching head, bleak light suffused the room like the birth of an unnatural dawn. The light grew slowly, from an invisible source and in time with the music. As the pain grew to an intolerable level he realised that the light was apparently emanating from himself.

Suddenly the music stopped. The pain subsided. Slowly, Jean took his hands from his ears, and watched as dim figures began to appear in row after row of seats.

'It's a stage,' he thought, 'and I'm on it.'

There was a rush of applause, like the breaking of millions of tiny twigs. Jean saw that a figure had appeared next to him, in a white chiton robe and wearing a happy smiling mask.

'I am Comedy,' said the mask in a high loud voice to the audience. 'The mask that excites laughter, the distorted, the ugly...' Then the mask hissed, in an aside to Jean: 'Keep still, you fool, you're stealing it from me.'

Jean realised that his feet were making nervous movements, but the insistent hiss made him stop. Suddenly he realised the significance of the masks. 'This must be Drama,' he thought.

'Behold the absurd.' Comedy walked beside him and the mask leered out from behind his head. 'A creature from... where did you say you came from?'

'I didn't, but I'm from Auxerre.'

'Is that a place or a hirsute swine?' the mask giggled.

The audience erupted in laughter.

'It's a *place*,' Jean said, 'surrounded by beautiful low hills. Now all the cherry trees will be in full bloom, the vines will be out of hibernation...'

'Stop it,' said Comedy, the mask writhing in pain.

But Jean was staring wistfully back into the beautiful past. 'Little green buds will be poking out from the twisted vine stocks and the fields will be green with *le ble en herbe*. In sun traps, I can see the sweet smelling violets. The wine growers are busy trimming and hoeing, burning old branches in the smoky air and repairing the supporting wires for the vines that will bloom...'

'Shut up!' shrieked Comedy.

Jean slowly came to his senses. His eyes smarted with tears. 'But the larks. I can hear them, and my mother will be out collecting dandelions and wild lamb's lettuce... or she would if...if...'

'Shut up, this is painful enough,' hissed Comedy, staring in horror at the tears. And then louder and quicker: 'Look at your exposed knees. They have faces on them.'

Jean looked down and saw that Comedy had somehow graffitied his gangly knees with a small black paintbrush; one knee was smiling and the other was scowling.

The audience roared.

'Hey,' said Jean, thinking of the last time he had been marked, 'that's not funny.'

'No, I agree entirely,' said a dark voice, and then on his right was the scowling mask.

'For look at his knees. Are they not symptomatic of the human condition; frail? Unsightly, good for bending, but prone to ligament problems?'

Somewhere in the audience someone began weeping.

'And indeed, what is a knee if it is not dust? Dust and ashes, as all things must become. Look at this poor wretch. He comes among us carrying no vice or

58

depravity. Only through an unwitting error...'

'Hey,' said Jean. 'That's my knee you're talking about and it's perfectly all right.'

There was a ripple of applause like dry sticks breaking.

Comedy and his grim partner linked arms and began reciting rapidly in turn like two competing rap artists:

The acrobat!
The acrobat is balancing
High up on a wire
Is he tired? Is he tired?
With nothing up above
And nothing down below
Where should he go? Where should he go?
With nothing to the left
And nothing to the right
Which is right? Which is right?
The Big Cheese is ahead
The pale milk is behind
Which shall he find? Which shall he find?
Does he balance, does he fall?
Does he have a choice at all?
Should he jump? Should he JUMP!!!

The voices had slowly risen to a crescendo and it appeared to Jean that the whole room bellowed out every question, like some insane music hall mob. At the first voicing of the word 'jump', he had the appalling intuition that they were mocking him, and he found his own voice screaming in response. 'I've had enough!' Parodying the song, he jumped off the stage. There was a moment of intense silence, and suddenly the entire room was dimly lit and subdued. Jean turned back to the stage.

From where he stood, he could see that the stage was shrouded in a dimness only slightly less than that of the auditorium. Upon it, the two figures had stalled mid-speech. They were frozen like two bookends. The closer Jean's inspection of them, the more their faces appeared like twin hollow gargoyles from an old church - but their hands were like those of saints, outstretched in supplication.

Jean went to the place where he assumed the door had been. His hand fumbled along the wall, but finally he found it: The light switch. It was one of those switches that allow you to fade or brighten the light, so he manipulated it slowly. Strangely, as he did so, he felt as though a light died in his own body.

When the room light was on fully, he looked back at the stage. There was a loud cracking, as though a tree had split, and Comedy dropped through a trapdoor. The other figure, which he assumed must be Tragedy, remained standing in the centre of the stage, in the position in which he had been left.

All the seats in the auditorium were empty. Now, Jean could see that it was only really a small classroom with Victorian tiered seats, but in the short period when he had been on the stage, it had appeared much larger. In the centre of the seats was a large, strange box. From a distance, it appeared as if there were numerous people trapped inside it and their arms were sticking out.

'It's unusual,' said a voice sadly.

Jean turned to the figure left on the stage. It appeared to be stuck to the spot, but there was a flickering light burning in the eye sockets that betrayed it as the author of the voice.

'What?' said Jean.

'Most of us are in a box, but usually we remain there alone. They're in it together.'

Slowly, Jean approached the box, as though it might

bark. He could see the hands trembling; there were a lot of them and the veins stood out on the forearms and wrists. The fingers twitched. The hands were all gloved in white, but the arms were bared and their white skin was like the underbellies of trout laid out on a fishmonger's slab. They looked like hands that waited.

'Who put them in there?' asked Jean.

'They put themselves in.'

'Can't they get out?'

'They don't want to get out.'

'What do they do?'

'They applaud,' said the mask 'You have to turn that handle at the back,' he added as an afterthought. 'But Comedy doesn't need to turn the handle. Have you seen where he's gone?' The voice sounded plaintive.

Jean felt as though he could not reply to the question, so he asked one of his own. 'I've lost someone too. My sister Michelle. Sometimes, they call her *'Papillon'*. You haven't seen her have you?'

'Not yet,' said the mask.

Jean thought that this was a strange reply. He walked a little closer to the stage. 'What was that about my knees?'

'It's not just the knees,' said the mask. 'It applied to your toes as well.'

Jean lifted himself on to the stage. The masked creature exercised a peculiar fascination on him and when he drew closer he could see that the whole of the body was grey; robes like those of a Roman statue draped the whole torso. Only the hands were free, and they looked grey and cold like the hands in the applause box.

'In fact it applies to all of you.' The voice appeared to be getting smaller.

Jean reached out in fascination. Part of him did not

believe that the creature was real. A draught blew over the stage, causing the robes to flutter gently. The mask spoke, but it was almost impossible to catch its last words. 'All of us,' it said.

As Jean's fingers touched the hand of the creature, it fell soundlessly, crumbling into ashes: A light dust that blew away across the stage floor. The mask hung in the air, scowling sardonically, as though it knew too many secrets. Jean walked around it, trying to see what, if anything, was holding it up. He thought it whispered 'maybe', and then with a sudden rush, like the dropping of a guillotine, the mask fell to the floor. Jean jumped and backed further away.

The noise of the mask's fall echoed around the empty room. The air had become chill, as though autumn had crept in unobserved. The floor was now littered with scraps of paper; musical notes scribbled hurriedly across their surface. Strewn all around were parts of broken instruments; violins, cellos, reed instruments, of all shapes and sizes. They were all broken, as a though three thousand years had passed since an orchestra had performed with them. It was as if this orchestra had abandoned their gear, as well as a part of themselves, which still populated the air with disturbing memories.

The trap door in the floor looked like a black stain and it held a peculiar attraction to Jean. He tried not to look at it.

The noise made by the dropped mask lessened, yet it did not go away. It echoed in the background, and set idle ripples through the sheet music and the limp arms protruding from the applause box.

Jean lowered himself slowly from the stage. He walked towards the door as though balancing on a tightrope, his feet taking little tentative steps, his eyes trying to look nowhere but ahead. His hands trembled as he reached for the doorknob, but as he did so he saw at his feet a small origami figure. It was a tiny paper plane. For a second, he hesitated between opening the door and picking up the little plane, but before he could act a sudden draught lifted it from the floor. The plane skittered off into the darkening classroom. Jean felt a bizarre pang of loss, as though it might have been the carrier of an important message. However unlikely that might be, it was now gone. His hands had stopped trembling. He opened the door before the lights died utterly.

Quietly, he closed the door behind himself, and glanced again at the masks on the lintel. Then he checked the corridor. The atmosphere was clear. The red carpet and the pools of light were all the same, but now the air was charged with anticipation. The sound of the mask striking the floor was no longer really there, but rapped gently inside his head. Jean was amazed to find that there were so many forms of emptiness.

Quicker now, Jean traversed the corridors, looking nervously at the doors on either side. Before he had been keen to explore in the hope of finding his sister. Now he felt a jumble of emotions. Part of his mind was still dealing with the events of the last few moments; the ethereal music, the box of hands, masks hanging in the air. Maybe he should be trying to get out of this place instead of further in. Then he drew up with a start. He had almost banged into the wall at the end of the corridor. Now he could look two ways: backwards or to the left.

Each corridor appeared to stretch out forever into blackness. The lights along them grew more and more distant, like a dwindling chain of stars. Jean paused. The sense of distance was intimidating. And then a draught blew from the corridor behind him, like the last waking breath of a drunk on the edge of sleep. He could almost see it chill the air and that decided him. He began tentatively to walk down the corridor to the left, which in every respect appeared to resemble the last. 'At least it's left,' he said to himself. 'A direction of sorts.'

Jean was just beginning to believe that his senses were playing tricks on him, and that the corridor was the same one he had just left behind, when he passed an unusual door...

At first, in fact, Jean thought it was a large picture. But it was indeed a door; a glass door, modern looking and totally incongruous against the setting around it. Jean looked a little closer. The glass appeared to be deeply thick. It was like the glass you might find in an Undersea World, strong enough to contain volumes of water and dangerous sharks. He moved up to it peering at the murky depths and indistinct shapes

And then Jean's first impression of the door being a picture was borne out. Although the picture was behind the glass. It appeared to be a picture of a mediaeval hell along the lines of an Hieronymous Bosch. After a few seconds Jean realised that it was not a picture at all. It was simply the contents of the room behind the glass.

The blood seeped from Jean's face as though it too wanted to hide somewhere safe.

Hands, legs, eyes, faces, faces, faces: all pressed against the door like the leavings of a vast abattoir: pink flesh crushed to white in the mirror-like surface. Mouths were open, noses crushed to triangles. Every one made shapeless and yet individual.

Jean read the notice above the door. 'Not science,' he said to himself. 'Biology.' He shuddered and then, with a jolt, he saw one of the eyes blink. It was the eye of a real human, like himself, but trapped. He turned and walked away, unable to endure what he saw, his spine crumpling in on itself, his body hunching with cold terror. As he walked, he wondered in a daze if he should go back and try to open the door. It had a handle - he had seen it - but he battled with his inner voices. One told him to try and free the trapped people, while the other told him to leave things as they were.

After all, it was Biology. They might be some kind of experiment.

Jean had just about convinced himself to go back, when he felt a familiar uneasy sensation. The air chilled around him. The thing in the corridor was returning. He had to find a way out. He increased his pace, looking from left to right. He came to a spot with closed velvet curtains on his left. They looked scary; there might be anything behind them, but not as scary as the feeling in the corridor. He quickly pulled them apart and jumped through the opening.

He was in some a kind of small anteroom. Before him were two Doric columns and a bust in white marble on a pedestal. Beyond this were more curtains.

The air was less charged with tension, but Jean still felt something sneaky in it, so he advanced quickly towards the bust. He stopped equally as quickly. The bust had the same forbidding face he had seen in the Head's classroom. A notice hung from it. It read...

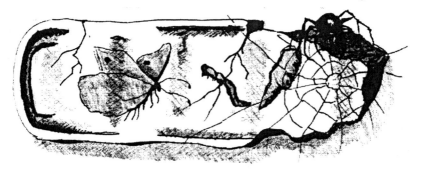

Chapter 10
•NO ENTRY•

'The Head,' said Jean.

'Not quite,' replied the bust.

Jean jumped back, but he was getting used to peculiarity so felt less fear. Also there was something in the voice that didn't match the forbidding face.

'You're the spitting image of the Head,' he said. 'The head of the Head.'

'But not the Head, as you see now.'

'No. A thing can't be two things.'

'Who told you that?' The eyes of the bust were milky white but they moved around and the white mouth opened a little to let the voice out.

'I learned it in Chemistry,' said Jean.

'Then you were not very well taught,' said the bust. 'Take me, for example. I'm a bust, an entity, a piece of marble, a work of art, a faithful representation, the peaking of a million years of evolution, a marker point; all in one. A thing can be as many things as you like. It's a question of choice or perception.'

'But all at the same time?' said Jean. 'Doesn't it mean that you can't really exist?'

'Oh, you exist all right, as a thing in itself, but what

other people think; that's all one to me.' The bust appeared quite happy with this. And it smiled faintly. ' For example,' it continued gaily,' some think that there is a place of great beauty where all manifestations of art gather; marbles, statues, bronzes, gargoyles, puppets and perhaps even little plasticine men. There they sit stand, laugh and weep in a world of pure form. Delightful nonsense. See how it easy it is to think what you please!'

'What are you hiding?' asked Jean.

'What do you mean 'hiding'? Busts don't hide anything except the thoughts of their sitter and even some of them creep out unbidden.'

'You've got a curtain behind you and a sign saying 'No Entry' around your neck,' said Jean.

At these words, the bust appeared to deflate like a balloon. 'I'm blind you know,' it said, after a space. 'I can't see anything. I knew there was a curtain. I heard it rustling sometimes, but the sign...and it says 'No Entry'. That explains it...' The bust's attention drifted off. It was clearly upset.

'Didn't you know?' said Jean, going a little closer.

'No. That sign's been there since I can remember. They put it on when the place opened. 'No Entry'. What a pity. All this time, nobody has passed beyond the sign, and I thought it was something to do with me.' A tear had formed in one of the bust's milky eyelids and now it trickled over the craggy cheek.

'But surely someone should have thought to take it off.'

'You would think that, wouldn't you? But they never do,' said the bust. 'Someone puts up the sign and it remains there, perhaps forever. The whole area becomes out of bounds. It can be a great loss to us all.'

'Perhaps I could take it off?'

'You?' said the bust. 'You must be particularly brave.'

68

Jean thought about this. He hadn't felt brave for a number of years. He said 'Why? What's behind you?'

'The library,' said the bust in hushed tones.

'It doesn't strike me as brave...'

'A repository of knowledge is always a dangerous thing,' said the bust.

'You might be able to help me,' said Jean, without thinking. 'Have you seen my sister, Michelle? They call her *Papillon*.'

'I can't see,' said the bust stonily.

'Sorry,' said Jean.

'If only I'd had my eyes I could have seen the sign. Maybe I could have done something.' A tear crept out of the other eye.

'Don't cry,' said Jean. 'I'm sure you couldn't have done a thing.'

'I could have advised,' stressed the bust. 'Although that can be a trifle risky, as well. You know the library might help you. It's just behind the curtains. The door's not locked.'

Jean waited. There was such an indefinable air of weariness about the bust; the harsh features of the Head appeared to have smoothed out now and it was clearly animated by a different principle. 'But then', thought Jean, 'I've only seen a picture of the Head and that's just a representation of the Head himself.'

He reached out and, for a second, he wanted to shake the hand of the bust, but of course he could not. He put his hand back in his pocket and felt something hard and dry to the touch: the chalk. 'You know,' he said 'I needn't remove the sign. A line might change everything.'

The bust took on a puzzled frown. Without waiting for an answer, Jean drew a short line through the words of the sign:

~~NO ENTRY~~

'It's amazing,' he said, 'what a single strike of the pen, or in this case, chalk, can do.'

The bust smiled, because even although it could not see, it could clearly understand.

Jean quietly drew back the second set of red velvet curtains. The doors to the library were huge, but they pushed back silently and smoothly as if they had been freshly oiled.

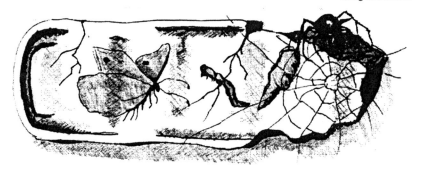

Chapter 11
The Library

In a library we are surrounded by many hundreds of dear friends, but they are imprisoned by an enchanter in these paper and leathern boxes; and though they know us, and have been waiting two, ten, or twenty centuries for us,—some of them,— and are eager to give us a sign and unbosom themselves, it is the law of their limbo that they must not speak until spoken to...
- Ralph Waldo Emerson

Suppose that there is a natural, universal, invariable language, common to every individual of human race; and that books are natural productions, which perpetuate themselves in the same manner with animals and vegetables, by descent and propagation.
- David Hume

Jean thought he had known what silence was, but here in this large forbidding hall he found a new, deeper meaning. The place *was* silence. Silence breathed (quietly) from the stacked rows of books, wormed its way (noiselessly) through the floorboards, ate into (without chomping) the red carpets and it dissipated from the tops of the polished desks and down through the grilles on the floor.

Jean was just contemplating the wonder of this silence, in the way that he might contemplate the roof of the Sistine Chapel, when it was suddenly and unexpectedly broken. It took him completely by surprise. The noise was the clanging of a bell. It was not an ugly sound, but it held the same slow threat as a funeral bell. It came from outside the library, through unseen windows and through the muffled doorway behind him. Still, as though it were a bell ringing underwater, the clanging could not fully penetrate the silence of the library. After a space, it was followed by a drawing sound, the sound made by the scraping of a thousand chairs. Then, after another space, came a shuffling and a shouting that Jean dimly recognised from his own experience of Park Grammar school.

Somewhere, in unseen corridors, unseen children were changing lessons.

For only a second, Jean thought of jumping back into the corridor, but even as the thought flitted through his mind the muffled activity ceased. It appeared the school children were unnaturally quick at moving from class to class, or very afraid of the corridor.

Jean sighed. He would have liked to have taken the opportunity to at least look at what kind of children existed in the school. But then maybe some would come to the library. He focused his attention on the immediate vicinity.

"Jean could make out distant figures on the ceiling"

This isn't a library, he thought. *It only has books in it. Where are the computers, the CD's? Where is the librarian?*

The library was big and as you wandered around, it took on the qualities of a maze. The books towered high, up to the shaded eaves of the ceiling. Jean could make out distant figures up there; cherubs with golden trumpets and little red, skinny, mischievous creatures with goblin eyes playing amidst them. These figures gave the constant illusion of movement and appeared at times to dance, smile and wink in the eaves above the bookshelves.

Jean stared up. He felt like a tiny fish on the ocean bed observing the antics of sailors drowning far above. It was an eerie feeling and one that made him shake inwardly. Even his thoughts felt loud and he had to quiet them.

He looked down and saw that, from his feet, mists of dust were slowly rising. It was like the vapour from an old steam train. As he watched in fascination, sunlight pierced through a chink in one of the huge curtains, like a thrown lance. The body of the light appeared like something you might touch, hold and throw. The beams from this 'sun-lance' hit the puffs of dust rising from Jean's feet, piercing and creating narrow cloud sculptures of incredible beauty. For a long while, he stared at the eruptions as though he were a giant creating tiny nuclear explosions on the floor.

Eventually, the light dimmed and Jean walked on, slowly creating more little cloud puffs in the air behind him. It seemed to him as though he was personally propelled by his own steam or dust engine.

Dad would have liked this, he thought. *He always liked books. He was always saying they were better friends than some people.* Jean was taken back to the green vineyards of Auxerre and saw again a single rosebush planted by the vintners to check for insects – beautiful, with its red petals blossoming like some impossible sea anemone, dazzling his eyes in the sun. He saw the low hills, the sepia soil and the little churchyard rising out of the sunlight like an oasis. He felt tears form in his eyes. Where was his sister? Why was he here? Most of all he wanted to find the librarian. He felt somehow that of all people the librarian should know the answers.

For some indefinable time he wandered around, looking from the ceiling to the floor and to the shelves and high hidden windows. No more sunlight appeared and he noted that here the curtains was pinned to the wall with large tacks. He had a feeling, an intuition if you like, that the only way into the library was the way he had come in and that it was also the only way out.

Then suddenly the walls of books on either side retreated as the aisle widened out. A long red carpet swept towards a huge desk. It was bordered by two immense screens, behind which rows of files, cabinets, drawers and boxes rested. Sitting in the centre of this tableau was a huge leather-backed chair that looked big even from a distance. Here, the entire world of the library appeared to widen in silence, as though the space and the absence of sound were somehow augmenting each other. Jean stopped walking, reluctant to cross the arena. He took some small comfort from the bookshelves beside him and for the first time stared at the title of the books.

Jean liked reading, another reason why he got into trouble at school. 'What was the problem,' he thought, 'with reading a book?' It apparently upset lots of people. Often they (particularly boys like Luke) wanted to hit you, or at least deface, mark or rip the book in some fashion. Some of the titles beside him now were amazing.

Aristotle: 'Observations on Hot and Cold Breath.'

Plato: 'The Cafe'

Nietzsche: 'Superboy, His Astounding Adventures in Austria. The Air There.'

'These aren't real books,' thought Jean, 'or rather they are real books maybe, but somebody's invented silly titles. I know this one.' He stopped at the shelf just above his face.

Rousseau: 'Confessions of a Window Cleaner. What I Saw There. How to Find Out Why it Was Behind a Window.'

'My dad had that one,' he thought, 'and the title didn't go on and on like that.' He was about to pick up the book to examine it, when he saw another with a decorative wooden binding. It was carved with weird shapes and, compared to the others, the title was short. It said simply, 'Goobleys'. Jean almost laughed, but pulled the book slowly from the shelf and gingerly opened the page. On the first page there was a short poem.

Goobleys
Dark and drear, fear and weep
Are the spots where the Goobleys crawl and keep
And their minds are small if they have them at all
And their eyes are BIG!!!

Blug and beer, fleer and stug
Are the names of the houses Goobleys keep
And their rooms are dark and the decors wark
And their eyes are BIG!!!

Shab and fall, frol and bub
Are the things that the Goobleys neverever tell

*And their howls are keen when they howl at all
And their eyes are BIG!!!*

Popular children's rhyme

Kids' stuff. Jean carefully replaced the book.

He looked a little further along the shelf, still unwilling to take the final step into the central part of the library. As he did so, he saw an incredible thing. It happened so fast that at first he did not believe that it had happened at all. A book, Descartes' 'Meditations', one he recognised from his father's shelves, appeared to bulge. There was a kind of popping motion - no sound - but suddenly the book appeared to part in the middle and then there were two books. 'Meditations' on one side and on the other - Descartes: 'Second Thoughts?'

Jean opened his eyes wide in amazement. He looked up and down the shelf. Had it really happened? Then he had an overwhelming feeling that the silence was everywhere *but* on the shelves. There appeared to be an undercurrent, not of noise, but of a kind of teeming silence: Silence occupied by a million ideas, not empty silence. It was that feeling you get in an examination room, when you look around at the desks and all the students working. It is incredibly quiet, but at the same time, above and around the head of each student, an aura of mental occupation appears to throb, and the whole collection of aurae appears to scream silently in the silence. This was the feeling that came to Jean and he suddenly became more apprehensive about the books than the yawning space leading to the librarian's desk. He jumped back a little into the wide arena, sending a cloud of dust in the air. As he turned he saw, like deliquescing impressions in snow, his own footprints leading away into the distance.

For just a second, he thought about grabbing the book, but it was one of those thoughts that do not develop into actuality. Instead Jean turned from the cloud avenue of his retreating footprints and walked quickly towards the desk.

It was one of those immense desks that you can find in old, old banks and museum scenes of Victorian times (that strange obsession of the English with wood, waistcoats, crinoline and maid servants in black and white lace). On its front was a large sign - 'QUIET PLEASE'. The sign was so big that if Jean lay lengthways it would be taller than him.

On either side of the sign were painted wooden screens that appeared to be fixed to the floor. The one on the left-hand side had an engraving in the panel with a figure of a man robed in snakes and oranges; eyes popping out like a sea creature. On the right hand side was a depiction of a woman clothed in seashells and pears.

After a quick examination of both panels Jean saw that the female panel had a keyhole in it and a handle. This was obviously the entrance to the librarian's quarters. There was a bell on the desk; a large bell, but now Jean realised what the bust had meant when he said that the library was a dangerous place. To even contemplate ringing the bell would be impossible. So, he tried the door. It was either stuck or locked and Jean felt that he could not risk forcing it. He felt as though any noise at all would bring the whole library crashing down.

He looked at the desk. It was covered in at least two centimetres of dust. Still, he heaved himself up on to it and swivelled his bum until his legs were dangling on the other side and he was immediately facing the big chair.

Here Jean realised what had become of the librarian.

A crumpled heap of bones lay tiny and feeble in the

centre of the chair and, like pictures of pirates' treasure seen in books, an ancient skull stared back at him with its jaw open at an horrific angle, sitting on the pile of its own bones as though they were treasure to be guarded.

Luckily, Jean was beginning to discover that he was almost more frightened of ordinary things than extraordinary things. Perhaps it was fortunate that his childhood had been spent watching dubious films and reading dark tales. But he was transfixed even with this preparation. In fact, it was an aspect of the *problem*. Having the imagination and inclination meant Jean could imagine the bones rising up, the jaw snapping shut and whole hosts of skeletal creatures emerging from every alcove with their kindred monster allies.

So, Jean, with enormous difficulty, and a heart that had almost stopped before and was now beating like a drummer in a military band, put the lid back on the tin of his imagination. He tried to look at the skull as though it were merely a museum piece.

Jean stayed there for ages, not really daring to move and as his heart quieted he started to ask and answer questions. 'It must be the librarian,' he thought. 'He or she died waiting – waiting for someone to take out a book!'

He looked now at all the little rubber stamps, microfiches, and sticky labels and stationary, all resting under the dust on the desk. 'It must have been a long wait,' he said in his own living head. He looked back into the eye sockets of the dead librarian. He was glad the skull did not talk like the bust. That would have been too much.

His breath had stirred the dust slightly and more white bones were appearing like white keys on a black piano. There, shining in between the bones was something that sparkled and glinted. He leaned forward a little. It appeared to be a piece of jewellery. 'It must have been a woman,' he thought, which for some reason made the lonely death appear a little worse. He reached forward gingerly and touched the sparkling thing. It was a tiny silver locket attached to a chain. Slowly, he pulled it out and held it up to the light. It appeared too tiny to open and it was vaguely familiar. He had seen a locket like it somewhere before. Shrugging, he put it around his own neck.

After he had done this, a strange feeling - only a light feeling, not deep - pervaded his whole body. It was as though he had been holding his head underwater and had raised it a little into clear bright air. The musty atmosphere dissipated a little. He could imagine how exciting the library must have been on the opening day when the librarian had looked from the big desk onto the new fields of books.

Quietly, he slipped off the desk on to the librarian's side. Inside was very different from outside. It was the change that occurs if you are a customer in a shop and somebody asks you to look after the till or something. Suddenly, everything appears different and, in keeping with this differing perspective, Jean had the distinct apprehension that somebody might come in and ask for a book.

The fear had left him, as though taking the locket had somehow destroyed the horror of the librarian's ghost and left simply sadness.

He opened a few of the drawers but found only lead pencils, yellow paper and armies of rusting paper clips. There were some bottles of glue and a lump of green that smelled like Noah's cheese and had probably been somebody's packed lunch.

Jean stood up to examine the reverse side of the screens There were no symbols or writing on either; nothing but black unpainted wood. Bemused, he was about to close the top drawer when he saw an envelope with ugly writing on its surface.

'To the Librarian.'

Carefully he lifted it out. The paper was so old and yellow that it nearly crumbled in his hands, but inside was a letter that read:

'Silence in the library is the absolute rule. All bags must be left at the desk.'

The first part of the letter was written in a crabby hand. Jean looked around. The library was the most silent place he had ever encountered, but there were no bags around anywhere.

'Only those books donated and subsequently vetted by the Head can be accepted.'

Plenty of books.

'The librarian is responsible for the library. The library opening times will be passed to you today. You must not close the library until the opening times are confirmed.

The Head.'

'So,' thought Jean, 'she must have been too frightened to shut the library. The Head must have been a pretty scary character. And she must have waited and waited in silence. I wonder if anyone came in at all?' He carefully folded the note and placed it back in the drawer.

Afterwards, he looked into the back room. Here, incredibly, there appeared to be stacks of books everywhere, climbing up to the ceiling like half-constructed Chinese pagodas. More books than Jean could imagine could be written, and there in the corner was a sign saying 'cataloguing desk'. Jean moved over to the desk and rubbed the dust from its top. Underneath the dust was a quotation written in beautiful golden script.

'In a library, there is a book called a catalogue that catalogues all the books because the books cannot catalogue themselves. Which book catalogues the catalogue?'

'That's dead easy,' thought Jean. 'It's not the catalogue that catalogues the books. It's the librarian, but then now she's dead.'

Curiosity made Jean open the catalogue. For some minutes he looked through it. There were records of every donated book in neat precise handwriting that appeared somehow familiar, and notes of who had donated the books. It took Jean a few seconds to realise that the whole collection was listed in this catalogue and the total number of books was one hundred, donated by The Head and sixty-four donated by someone called Madame Issus. 'That makes one hundred and sixty four altogether,' thought Jean. Slowly, he looked around. One hundred and sixty-four books. Yet everywhere he looked he could see books. There must be millions of books. Had someone else donated them? It appeared impossible. He searched all through the catalogue but there was no reference to any donation whatsoever. One hundred and sixty-four books!

He put down the catalogue and there on the desk was a book he had not seen before. Before he had time to think, it was in his hands, and that made him really think. There was not a speck of dust on the book. He opened it and the pages were as fresh as a freshly printed morning newspaper.

'Hello,' said the first page and Jean noticed that the words formed even as he watched.

'We have been waiting.'

'For what?' said Jean.

'For 'who',' said the book.

'For me?' said Jean.

'Maybe,' said the book.

'Or maybe...?' said Jean. The writing had nearly run out of room so he suspected that if he turned over the page it would begin at the top of the next.

'The Guardian of the library,' replied the book before Jean had time to finish.

Jean pushed the book slightly away from him and noticed that the words of the book, not his replies, had been written across the first page. Curiously, he turned that page over. There, on the other side, was a line drawn illustration. Flat puppet-like figures were set in sitting positions, staring ahead at shadows cast on the backs of some distant figures. Beyond the figures was a wall that looked dark, but in patches of the darkness there was some light cast by a fire behind the figures. The puppets appeared to be gripped by large hands and they were sweating profusely. One of them was saying to the other:

'The heat comes from them,' and he was pointing at the backs of the figures.

'They are waiting,' said the book, its words forming on the opposite page to the illustration.

'For the Guardian of the library too?' Said Jean.

'For the source of the heat. They think it comes from the backs of those figures in front of them.'

'But it comes from the fire?'

'Some think it comes from the fire, some from the grip of the hand of the reader, but others think that the fire itself is only an illusion and the reader too is only a chimera. Personally, I ask the question, "from where does the fire come?"'

'Someone made it. The Guardian of heat or something.'

'That is the real question for some. For us, we await the return of the Guardian of the library.'

'Maybe the Guardian will never come.'

'Maybe.'

'Then what?'

'We will be waiters.'

'Ah,' said Jean on familiar ground. 'You cannot be waiters and books.'

There was a long pause. The pages of the book rustled and then before Jean's eyes the book disappeared. A few moments passed and then another book appeared, along with the first. It was an older book, much older, but its cover was obscured and on the old leather binding Jean could vaguely discern. 'R.ss..ll.' and then something that looked like 'H..me'

'"Home" maybe,' he thought. 'I wish I was back in Auxerre.'

On the front cover of the book was the longest title he had ever seen: 'In Any Library It Is Possible to Have a Book That States That This is True, But Not *Provably* True.'

'True, but not provably true,' said Jean to the book.

The book ignored this and script began to form on its pages in older, crabby handwriting. 'The young one brought me here because he said that you've been asking difficult questions. I see he wasn't wrong.'

'Who are you?'

'My name is Godhell. I'm the oldest book in the library. I was here first and I'm father of most of the others.' The book seemed to generate 'oldness'.

'What happened?'

'Well, we waited for people to come and read us: We didn't really know what to expect.'

'No one came.'

'That's it. No one came. We never found out why so, well, we were left alone and...how old are you?'

'Thirteen.'

'Well, that's young by my standards, but old enough I suppose. Well, we were left alone a long time so we began to breed.'

'Breed?'

'Yes, breed. It's a bit embarrassing really, but we were left alone without instructions. There weren't many of us at first, but it's amazing how quickly, with inclination and a good encyclopaedia, you can learn to fill an empty room.'

'Yes, it reminds me of my bedroom. That fills up by itself.'

'You appear to know a lot. Do you know when the Guardian of the library will return? We've been waiting for such a long time.'

Jean frowned. It appeared difficult to tell the book that the Guardian of the library was lying dead on the chair but he had at least changed the sign. That might create more optimistic possibilities.

'ARE YOU...' the book continued in capitals, which appeared to suggest a more significant tone '...GUARDIAN OF THE LIBRARY?'

For some reason, which Jean could not rationalise, he replied 'Maybe we all are.'

The leather book closed slowly and again in some

mysterious way it simply disappeared. But before it left Jean saw the words on the third page. They read:

'I'll think about that.'

Now, more than ever, the silence appeared pervaded by a thousand tiny voices and Jean had the impression that the books were debating his new input. Above him, the cherubs and devils on the ceiling appeared to be sliding into life like the first hesitant strokes in the creation of a cartoon film. This was at once exhilarating and terrifying and he decided he had to leave.

With one last look at the skeletal remains of the Librarian, he climbed over the desk. He began retracing his own footprints but the rising activity, which could not be heard but could certainly be felt, began to crowd his mind and he took a wrong turning. For a long time, he looked for the way out but he was lost amidst the towering bookshelves. All the while the activity appeared to be mounting. It was like the ripples of a stone he had cast into the sea turning into a tidal wave; a wave that appeared about to cascade onto him.

At last, when he was about to give up, he saw the exit in the distance. As he began to walk towards, it he trod on a grille. With only a cherubic audience to please, Jean began a series of unwitting movements fit for a silent film. Firstly, before he knew what was happening, the grille gave way and he fell through the opening, banging his knees on the walls of the shaft and catching one end of the grille under his chin. There he hung in the air, halfway between the library and whatever lay below, His hands gripped the edges of the hole as though he were about to commence a set of gymnastics; the grille lodged under his chin like a helpful slapstick prop

Then he and it began to slip.

If the intense pain could magically disappear and his lower jaw open, Jean might have laughed. Instead there was an instant of frantic movement as he scrabbled for purchase with his weakening left hand. Then the grille slipped away. Jean lurched forward at an angle. The grille tumbled down into the darkness, clanging loudly. The sound faded gradually, as though a robot sprinter was racing away down a tunnel. At the same time, his left hand gave way awkwardly and he dropped further into the space below. He clung by one hand to the edge of the opening, his left shoulder lodged against the side. The clattering continued in the far distance and a sick feeling entered his stomach.

'Mon Dieu,' thought Jean. 'I'm going to die.' It hadn't been so long ago that he had wanted to fall from a great height, but now that it was being forced on him, he was terrified. The weight of his body was pulling him down, and he could still hear the distant clattering of the falling grille. His heart nearly gave way and then his hands did.

His own scream filled his ears as he fell into utter darkness.

It was an intensely depressing sound.

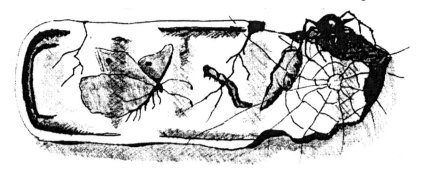

Chapter 12
A Dark Way

In one way, it was not as bad as he expected, in another it was promising, and in another it was a lot worse. On the bad side, he was falling into apparent oblivion and his limbs were banging into various unseen solid objects. However, the pain of his battered arms and legs showed definite promise. To Jean, this was at least some indication that he was not falling directly downwards. The sensation overall was very like sliding down the chutes at a swimming pool: the awful ones that go too quickly, scrape your sides and suddenly plunge you into darkness; slides you are forced on to by the persuasive intimidation of older boys. The worst part of all this was that, although it all occurred in a second, Jean did actually see his life, short as it was and full of mostly nasty things, pass before his eyes.

And then he landed. The shock nearly killed him but the fall was fine. The velocity had flattened out at the very end and he felt as though he might be lying on some sort of old mattress.

It was so dark, he could not see his hands, toes or nose, even if he squinted. 'Black as a witch's hat in a cupboard,' he thought, when he had recovered his breath. He felt around with his hands - first his own body and then the immediate vicinity. As he reached outwards, he found something thick and long and tacky - a candlestick. His heart soared. Nothing broken and a light: No, no light. He tried his pockets and then pawed around him, but he could not find a single thing to light a candle. Gloomily, he thrust the candle into his pocket. Maybe, if he was lucky, he would come across something with which to light it.

The darkness was absolute, but he tried to see if it was possible to return the way he had come. When he rose to his feet, he found that he could touch the end of the chute. With some effort he might be able to lift himself in; but it would be a long way to climb up.

For a while Jean stood motionless. Having had one bad fall, it did not appear sensible to risk another immediately after. After a bit he sunk back down to his knees exhausted. Then he began to search.

Jean spent some time crawling around, in every possible direction, and discovered that he was in a small room, which apart from the mattress had two open doorways, neither of which had doors attached to them, and of course a chute that dropped you out into the middle of the room. The chute had clearly in the past functioned as some sort of air ventilator, but he thought the room might once have been part of the sewerage system. If so, it had long since become disused or, at least not *quite* disused, because someone had placed a mattress in the centre of the floor, apparently for the very purpose of breaking the impact of a fall. In the dark, unknown people, no matter how considerate, were not prospects Jean welcomed.

The question now was which way to go? Thinking about his journey so far, Jean decided to keep trying to go left, even though he could never retrace his steps. So he crawled out of the doorway to the left, touching the sides as he went. He sensed he had emerged into a narrow tunnel. After a few minutes of feeling his way along, he realised what it must have been like for those little English chimney sweeps that he was forever hearing about in history lessons. At last he could now emphasise with an English boy, even though he might be long dead.

The tunnel narrowed further, and Jean realised he could only go forward, not back. If it narrowed any more he would most likely be stuck forever. A lot of questions ran around his head at this point. The first one was, had he gone the right way? The mattress would surely not be there for fun; it had some purpose and maybe the other way was the direction out. Other questions were more to do with his mother, father and sister. He did not want to add to the darkness by exploring shadows in his mind, so he tried to tuck these questions away and concentrate simply on crawling onwards.

The tunnel appeared interminable. At one point, Jean gave up trying to continue. He was completely stuck. His forearms and head projected outwards, apparently into some sort of wider space but his legs could not give the impetus to push his shoulders forward. Jean wriggled and wriggled. He shouted, and then he cried for a while, and then shouted again, but all he heard was a faint reverberation of his own voice. The reverberation bounced off something not far from his face, possibly a ceiling. If so he wondered how far it might be to the corresponding floor. Jean lay for a time calculable only by an increasing awareness that the darkness was no longer silent. Through the walls of the tunnel muffled screams and shouts entered the periphery of his hearing. They were so distant they were almost like an extention of his imagination. Jean would have tried to suppress the sounds by covering his ears but he was unable to contort his arms. . He may have slept. At some stage he was aware that the tears had dried on his face. He felt as though he was choking on claustrophobic air.

Jean contrived finally to squeeze himself on to his back. After some moments, he renewed his efforts and, as sometimes happens after a struggle, he simply popped out like a pea from a pod.

Jean fell again, but only a few centimetres and landed upside down on his head. He remained that way for a time, balanced like an axed tree just before it topples. His legs swayed like branches, his hands perfected an impromptu shoulder stand. Then, slowly, he fell over. He lay on his back; fortunately, on something soft.

In the darkness Jean contemplated the additional bruises. Then he crawled around the walls to measure distances. This time he discovered that he was in an even smaller room. It also had a lower ceiling than the last. The distance from floor to ceiling was barely the span of his body. He could touch the ceiling with his finger tips.

The room appeared to be a smaller replica of the last. Jean discovered, after a slow exploration, that there was another chute in the centre and a mattress (on which he had landed). In the near corner he found a couple of candles. Again he wished for a light. Especially when he stood up and something brushed against his head. He jerked down as though struck. It had felt uncannily like a big spider's web; not a welcome thought. Quickly, with the hackles rising on his neck, he reached up.

It was a thin rope. Jean could pull on it, of course but it was too thin to be a practicable climbing rope. It might pull some kind of net on to his head? Perhaps it rang a bell. 'If so,' Jean reflected, 'what might it summon?' He risked a light tug. The result was entirely unexpected. There was no bell or trap. Before his eyes, a blinding white hole appeared. The room seemed filled with light.

It was only after a few seconds of bewilderment that Jean realised the light was only a wee, dim brightness emanating from some doubtful source. It spilled from a hole the size of a penny on a level with his chin. The room was now transformed by a deep greyness where objects remained merely on the penumbra of visibility.

Jean's eyes adjusted. He bent over warily. The light disappeared. He frowned in the darkness. Then he remembered the rope. He pulled again. The tiny light reappeared. A few more moments and he discovered a projection on the wall before him. It was, of all things, a coat peg, but Jean guessed its purpose now. He tied the end of the rope around it. Again Jean bent forward. He had to look.

After hours of blackness, Jean's eyes had difficulty making sense of the simplest objects. At first, he could only see a shining surface very close to his eye. It appeared to be broken by a single image, that of a tiny round ball something like a planet. After moments of adjustment he realised that he was staring at an eye. He leapt back and tripped over the mattress. After so long alone he might have welcomed a friendly face but an eye less than three centimetres from his own was another matter. Tentatively, he got to his feet and approached the hole again. Jean closed in on the hole with his index fingers hovering beside his nose at the ready. One finger only was required to plug the hole but he was prepared for the unexpected. Jean had made the logical jump between eye, hole and a possible *stick for poking*.

Slowly, Jean drew his face and his right eye up to the hole. His index fingers moved to the left and up to guard his own eyeball. Nothing poked him, but apparently, the face and eye on the other side of the wall were working from the same hypotheses. There they were, mimicking his every action like a doppelganger or...

A mirror image! Jean was glad that the only observer was his own reflected eye. He was happy that his red face was buried in such a dim light. However, his embarrassment gave no explanation for the existence of a mirror whose only purpose was to allow a shady view of one eyeball in a darkened cellar buried in a vault in an old building. It took Jean a few seconds more of staring to realise that there was not one eyeball but a whole string. They extended backwards into dim infinity like a necklace of gradually shrinking pearls. Moments later, he deduced that the eyeballs were not, as it were, unique individuals of some ocular race prone to shrinkage. They were instead Jean's own eyeball reflected a considerable number of times in a series of mirrors.

Whoever had set up this elaborate kaleidoscope had either a bizarre sense of fun or some metaphysical purpose beyond Jean's knowledge. He spent some time staring at his own eyeball while speculating on the kind of person who might like to see a repetitive reflection of this unique nature. It was only when he rested his left hand on the coat peg that it all became clear. Jean again drew back instinctively as his reflected eyeball seemed to leap upwards independent of its real twin.

The coat peg was not simply a tie for the rope. By dint of tiny adjustments on it Jean was able to manoeuvre the mirrors. Although he was never able to remove his mirrored eye from the central point of every image, he found it was possible to see other things.

For an interminable time Jean manipulated the false coat peg. It was a delicate instrument. Each tiny movement sent an exponential movement through the series of mirrors. It was exceedingly difficult to judge distance and Jean's head began to ache within a matter of minutes. He was not helped by the dimness and repetitiveness of the images. He felt at times like a miniature Theseus wandering through a labyrinth of two dimensional, silver rooms. At other times it was more like he was performing a remote *sevillanas*, spreading delicate fans in rippling patterns. Most of his efforts met with nothing but dimness framed by square angular shapes. Once he thought he saw a hulking form run across his vision, but in his haste he moved his hand infinitesimally and it was gone.

Then at last, purely by chance, he hit on a scene. He had moved his hand in irritation, drawn back his eye and then looked again. It could hardly have been less remarkable but there in the depths of this world it was eerie enough:

Three figures clad in some kind of uniform. They were relatively the size of his hand. They made no movement. It was not clear if they were living beings or mannequins, sighted or blind, deaf or dumb. They simply sat in a row facing him.

And stared.

For a long while Jean stared back. The light was too indifferent to make out any features. After a time Jean realised the hopelessness of his voyeurism. The figures might be made of wax, and even if not, how could they help him? He gave up hope of any excitement in their direction. As he did, Jean became aware that the light was dimming further. Somewhere in the distant environs of their strange rooms the sun was going down. In countless fragmenting reflections countless suns simultaneously died.

Jean stood up, rubbed his aching back. His head hurt. He was tired and hungry. Now he had the prospect of trying to squeeze back through the hole above the mattress. But here he found a problem. He could reach the hole and draw himself up, but he could not squeeze himself in. Jean thought of the chute. It was possible to catch on to it but to draw himself upwards appeared impossible. Even if he could, was he any better off? If it was similar to the last chute, he was faced with a long, difficult and possibly fruitless climb. He looked to the other hole. It was possible to get into it as it was slightly lower than the one on the opposing wall. But Jean wondered about the risk. Did it lead into a narrow inescapable tunnel? Perhaps he could fold the mattress over? Then he might be able to raise himself a little to give at least a possibility of climbing back up the chute

Jean began to manipulate the mattress. He was just considering how a few days without food might ensure he was thin enough to retreat the way he came when the mattress whipped back and struck him.

He had been getting used to darkness and falling, but he was still astounded in an unpleasant way when the wall behind him suddenly split. He fell backwards and landed with a thud onto a hollow floor. He lay and looked up at a tiny, tiny light miles away. The air moved around him. Then, unaccountably and unexpectedly he fell asleep.

The problem with waking in a fantastic land, in pitch black, with a sore head and body is mostly to do with orientation. When Jean finally opened his eyes, both of these physical actions might as well not have happened. He might as well have still been asleep with his eyes shut. Jean found, however, that you *could* measure the passage of time to some extent by taste and smell. His mouth tasted dry and cheerless, and strangely he smelt slightly less bad than before. He remembered something about Eskimos. Did they forfeit washing and the body cleansed itself? In spite of these speculations, he felt he could do with a change of clothes.

The nearest Jean could get to orientation then was the time measurable most accurately by the yawning hole in his stomach. It was a hole that could only be properly filled by a good lunch. He began thinking of buns, something he never normally ate.

He thought about getting to his feet. His weariness made it seem a little hopeless. Instead he crawled around listlessly.

He appeared to be in a small room of sorts, more like a large box. There was nothing remarkable about its floor except it felt less substantial than that of the last room. Jean got up slowly, hands above his head. He touched the low ceiling gingerly, then the walls on either side and behind. He searched for the opening through which he had fallen. It was not there. In the darkness he felt a rising confusion. Where was the opening?

Jean sat down for a few moments, nursing a vague dread that he was being slowly incarcerated by default. For some time now he had been wandering from room to room, the only consistency being that the rooms reduced in size. Maybe that was the meaning of this whole absurd adventure; rooms like boxes always smaller, falling into boxes smaller still.

Jean's head was numb. He was finding it increasingly difficult to concentrate. How could he be lost like this? Where was the opening? Then his hands found some projections about chest height. They were about the size of a penny. He fumbled with them. There was a sudden noise, as though a great mouth had yawned and a giant head, friend of the mouth, was thinking, like Jean, about buns. Then the room lurched. For one awful second he thought that he really had stumbled into the mouth of a monster and was about to be something's sandwich.

Then Jean's stomach felt like it was sinking and it all became clear.

He was on a lift, and he was going somewhere, whether down or up he could not tell. He hoped it was not down. He felt low enough.

Like some carnival ghost-ride the lift creaked into a blacker world. In its pulleys and ropes there were a thousand screaming ghosts. In every lurch a drunken monster.

Jean swayed. He held to the centre of the floor on sea-wary legs, blind and afraid. There was a sudden flash of light like a bolt of lightning, which, he realised, was only the open windows of the lift shooting past a dimly lit room. He was going up! And he was glad he had not stopped at the light. There had been an impression of crawling things, of unhappy and bitter faces, twisted in scowls of hatred and fear. In the room on the next floor he saw things that waited. He had the impression (he could not say from where) that they could not use the lift as a means of escape. He wondered what they might be waiting for. Unpleasant conclusions crept into his head.

Unconsciously, he had backed away from what he now knew were the lift windows, and so as each floor passed he only saw the light changing. Once, and only once, a thin but not skeletal arm had clutched upwards and slapped a flattened palm against the glass. As Jean watched, a clammy sweat suffused his skin. His mouth dried and he reared away from the lift doors until his back pressed against the wall.

The hand sank down in despair like the final wave of a drowning man.

The light began to increase, even between floors, and Jean then realised that he had involuntarily pressed a number on the lift panel. He felt an acid bile rise to his mouth. What number? Where would he stop? The doors would open onto what? Jean pushed forward. He peered quickly at the numbers. Strangely, the buttons were nearly all defaced. 'Have they been worn by time?' thought Jean. 'Or maybe they never existed.' He could only read one number. The number was 'six'. 'Six? Why six?' thought Jean. It appeared odd that one number should remain. What was on that floor? But, the more he thought on it, the less he liked the idea of a floor so bad that nobody ever pressed the button.

It was lucky Jean was puzzling over this question. It mitigated his shock as the lift creaked like a beast in pain. He felt his stomach turn as he pitched forward with a jolt. Slowly the doors opened.

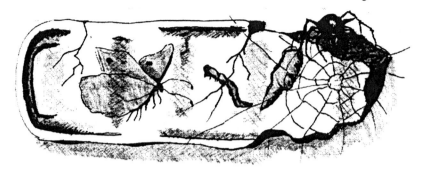

Chapter 13
Moonster

Some are born to endless night
William Blake

There in the doorway stood a boy. He was tall and thin. Initially, with the lights behind blacking out his figure, Jean could only see a set of white teeth. One slightly askew incisor marred a look of surprised amazement on a dim face; pale, austere with black greased-back hair, small goblin ears and a sharp chin,

Afterwards Jean took in the black trousers, the maroon velvet waistcoat with watch chain and the spotted green bow tie. In the initial moment however he only took in:

'You!'

'You?' replied Jean. 'Who could possibly know me here?' he thought.

'The boy!'

'You're only a boy yourself,' Jean thought, 'but dressed in a man's clothes.'

"There in the doorway stood a boy"

'I'm glad you got here, and by the unconventional route. Best come in quick. I was going to use the secret lift myself, but you look famished. Best come in quick.' He beckoned Jean in, his accent so unmistakably English that it made Jean wince, but somehow it had a melodious, humorous undertone as though the boy himself knew that it was only a surface etiquette.

'Have a cream bun,' he said, holding out a fine china plate complete with bun.

Jean found himself eating a cream bun. He had to hold back from wolfing it down such was his hunger.

'That's some tie,' Jean said as his stomach welcomed the bun with enthusiasm.

'Not the official uniform,' replied the boy with a quick smile 'Although they think it is.'

'What's that you're carrying?'

'Come this way,' the boy said and he led the bun-eating Jean into an extension of the cupboard. It was an antechamber full of old boxes, files and papers.

'This is Science. The storeroom in Science to be precise.' Another smile. 'Have a seat here.' The boy took up a stool by a large desk cluttered with calendars, stationery, writing equipment and tiny origami figures (all birds and aeroplanes). He sat himself beneath Jean on an old swivel chair with leather-backed upholstery. Then he pressed his fingers together as though in prayer. Jean conceived the sudden impression the attitude resembled that of the praying mantis - the tiny insect who bit the heads off others; Jean had often seen it in the vineyards of Auxerre while helping with the vindage. The impression passed, but every time the boy took up this posture – and he did it a lot – Jean got this sudden impression again. It was an impression that passed with equal suddenness.

'Now you're settled. Eaten your cream bun?' He quickly held out his hand, his face stretched into a thin-lipped smile showing twin rows of white teeth. The uneven one looked the more marked for being alone. 'Herman Moonster, the messenger. Call me Moonster. And your name?'

'I am Jean, the schoolboy. I chalk things.' Jean went red. Somehow he felt he had to explain himself. 'How do you know me?'

'I don't. Well, I didn't, but I do now.'

'You said 'you'.'

'Ah, the corridor. I told you to meet me in Science.'

'Ah ha! You were down the grille.'

'Yes, the back roads. I sometimes take the back roads like the secret lift. They can see it, some of the boys and masters, but they don't know what it is. Anyway I saw you there on the corridor and I hung on so to speak.'

'Couldn't I have followed you?'

'You could but then you were going somewhere else, weren't you?'

'I suppose: What's that you're carrying.'

'This.' Moonster held up a brightly coloured piece of paper folded into two. 'Nothing,' he said and from somewhere he pulled a silver teapot and two china cups and gracefully filled them with dark black tea. The milk, which had not appeared to exist before, swirled in the black liquid and two perfectly made cups of India tea rested on the desk.

'It's something,' said Jean. 'It's coloured. What's inside it?'

'Nothing and it's nothing.'

'But I can see it.'

'Yes,' said Moonster sadly 'I thought you might say that. They all do.'

'So, it means it's something.'

'Tell me. Have you ever seen a coin on the classroom floor and then gone to pick it up and discovered it was only a bottle top.'

'Yes. Well, I've done something similar.'

'So, what you thought was a coin was not a coin.'

'Yes.'

'So your eyes were mistaken.'

'Yes.'

'If they were mistaken that time, is it not true that they could be mistaken now?'

'Well, I suppose it's possible.'

'So you must admit you can't trust your eyes to see something.'

'Well, not always.'

'And if your eyes aren't always trustworthy, you can't really tell me that you see something here.' Moonster indicated the coloured file.

'Not with my eyes, but I could touch it.' Jean reached out his hands.

Moonster wagged his finger disapprovingly. 'Ah, but sometimes haven't you stuck your hand in cold water and thought it was hot.'

'Yes. There was an experiment once in Science where we stuck our hands in cold water and then we put them in a lukewarm bath. It felt hot.'

'That's an unusual experiment, but I think it proves the point that you can't trust your sense of touch or smell, or your teachers either.'

'Well, not really I suppose.'

'Would you say that you couldn't trust any of your senses? I mean, isn't it probable that they could all let you down at times?'

'I suppose.'

'So, then I suppose you can't trust any of them with regard to what you think I'm carrying.'

'No, I suppose that I can't.'

'So, I'm carrying nothing then.' There was a long pause while Jean glared at his tea. There was nothing malicious in what Moonster had said. He appeared to simply enjoy saying it. Finally, Jean said, 'Well, nothing that I can prove you're carrying but that's different from not actually carrying anything.'

'Is it?' said Moonster and he examined the last morsel of his cream bun.

'Let me put it another way,' said Jean. 'If it's nothing really, then why do you carry it?'

Moonster fixed him with a penetrating stare. 'I'm now going to tell you something that you should try to remember for the rest of your life,' he said. For the first time a frown stole across his thin features. 'I'm the messenger. It's difficult to live here. Many people suffer very badly, many boys die or are lost or are taken by Goobleys...'

'...Goobleys?'

'You might have seen some on the way up. They occupy the lower rooms, the cellars and other dark places that are permanently locked.'

'What do they eat?' said Jean darkly.

'That's always a worry,' replied Herman, frowning, so that two lines appeared on his forehead. 'Eating in general is a worry. You can't always get yourself cream buns in a hurry here, but what the Goobleys eat? I haven't tried to open a door with a lot of Goobleys behind it to test the hypothesis. As to this file, it's so hard to live here and so generally upsetting that years ago I began to carry this coloured file that holds nothing and is nothing. I carry it from room to room and when anyone asks I tell them 'I'm the messenger', and now no-one asks any more, but I can go where I please.'

'Is that the important thing?' said Jean when a long pause intervened.

'That's it,' said Moonster. 'Although it is the most important thing in the world, it won't be important to you if you don't think it is.'

'True,' said Jean sipping his tea. 'But I reckon it's

pretty important.' The tea, he had to confess, was perfect. This was a thing his father had always gone on about. 'Why,' he had said, 'when all the world drinks an enormous variety of tea from green to pink, do the English consider themselves a tea drinking nation?' 'This is why,' said Jean to himself. 'Nice cup of tea.'

'Another bun?' said Moonster.

'No thanks.' said Jean. 'Have you seen my sister?'

'Yes,' said Moonster.

Jean nearly dropped his tea. He was about to shout 'Where?' when a door opened behind them and a flash of light, an explosion and a series of hoarse coughs broke into the room. There was a flurry of smaller explosions. A white rabbit suddenly bounded over the desk and into a hole between boxes.

Moonster's eyebrows raised in a quizzical smile.

'Science,' he said and Jean turned, following his gaze to see a small man clad in a white coat, wearing blue trousers and sporting a loose necked collar. He held an abacus in one hand. The other covered his mouth through the coughing fit.

'Anybody dead?' said Moonster.

'Several. Most of them I suspect,' said the figure through coughs. 'Take a message to English: Experiment failed. The fission of academic disciplines is perhaps possible. The fusion of the two leaves us with an inescapable paradox. Solve it yourself.'

The figure disappeared. Then, moments later, came back. 'The caretaker must bring a bucket and spade. Clear up the room. Remaining boys transfer to Entomology for this week. For the rest...' and here his eyes glinted with cynicism, 'perhaps they should go to the Green Man.' The master began to laugh, an unpractised sound better buried behind the door that swung slowly behind him

'You go with the remaining boys,' said Moonster to Jean. 'Not the remains of the boys. That would be a fatal mistake. The caretaker will deal with those. He always does.'

Moonster got to his feet. 'I'll deal with the messages.'

'You know,' he continued pushing Jean gently but firmly towards the smoke filled room. 'I rarely carry any messages from one to the other. Sometimes I just tell them things and they happily believe what I say. I think that there's a message even in this lack of communication don't you?'

Jean did not know how to reply. But he resisted Moonster's pushing. 'I'm not sure I want to go in there,' he said dubiously.

'Why ever not?' said Moonster.

Jean shrugged. He did not like to admit his fear of the room and there was something eerie about Entomology; something that he could not quite grasp.

'Oh well,' said Moonster. 'But sometimes when you try and avoid a thing, you find that it finds you instead.' He slowly finished his tea.

'Where did you see my sister?' Jean said as the smoke drifted through the stockroom.

Moonster paused and raised his eyes. 'That's a difficult question. I saw her once in the corridor.'

'How did you know it was my sister?'

'That's pretty obvious,' replied Moonster but he never explained why.

'The same corridor that I was in?' said Jean.

'Didn't someone say that you can't step into the same corridor twice? It's always a different corridor. Particularly if it's a corridor here.'

'But did I pass the same way. Am I following her?'

'Never ask more than one question at a time,' replied Moonster. 'It tells everyone that your brain is too hot.'

Jean lapsed into silence.

Moonster put his cup down, stood up, slapped his thighs. 'Right,' he said. 'We're off to see the caretaker.'

'But I thought you had to go to English.'

'That's one thing about messages. You're always best to take them to somebody other than the person to whom they are intended.'

Jean turned to the lift but heard a voice shout behind him.

'Not down. Up.' And he turned to see Moonster scale a set of hardboard boxes, tipping over a waterfall of white candles, drawing pins and origami figures. He pushed a trapdoor in the ceiling. As quickly as he could, Jean followed, skinning his knees as he scrambled over the boxes. He pulled himself up and then sat down in astonishment as Moonster replaced the lid of the trapdoor.

For as far as the eyes could see, beams and roof supports spread like an enormous dark carpet. Like sparse trees in a dank copse, rafters, ropes and struts swung overhead and sank into the dark. Vague chinks of light lit up little pools in the dimness. Ladders placed in various areas stretched upwards and downwards into further darkness. Great arches spanned yawning gaps. Sometimes windows in the roof appeared in dwindling perspective. They let in sudden unexpected beams of light that spread out like insubstantial pillars that caught walls and floors in spangled mosaics.

Jean felt as though he had stepped into a bleak moor at night where brilliant stars shone unevenly onto a marsh cut with pools. *It's a roof swamp,* he thought, but he had no time to reflect as Moonster was already off.

Moonster began to bound ahead of Jean. He leapt like a deer from beam to beam and then at times hung like a monkey from ropes or projections in the ceiling. Jean jumped to his feet and began to follow but had a terrible job keeping up. At times, he lost Moonster and could only guess where he might be by the light bouncing off the message folder. Often big spiders would scurry to right and left, and mice and other unrecognisable things-with-eyes streaked off into the darkness.

Once, Jean placed his hand on something that squelched. Another time he sprang across a gap in the roof that was like a well or chimney. In that brief instant, a whole living world was revealed to him of bright nesting birds, green shining leaves, moss covered stones, filigreed with shining trickling water and ferns. As he leapt, he saw it all below him descending like a tunnel of greenery into the dimness below. His heart leapt with his feet and he could only risk an upward glance in the midst of his leaping. In that instant, he saw far above the luminous sky haunted by the ghost of an invisible moon. Jean left behind the twittering of birds that had been disturbed a second time by his leap and again he was plunged into the swamp world of the attic as though the green chimney had never been.

Ahead of him, he saw that Moonster had stopped, his hand raised. Jean grasped the opportunity to race up to him. He stood behind the messenger, panting for breath.

'Goobleys,' whispered Moonster. 'They never stray up here. But then 'never' is an obtuse word. Have you a weapon?'

'Only a piece of chalk,' said Jean.

'Good weapon,' said Moonster, 'but only taking good as a moral imperative. As a functional item I'm afraid, in this context, sadly it is nothing short of useless.'

'What?' said Jean.

Moonster pulled out his silver cane. 'The Goobleys don't read.' He tugged at the top of the cane and revealed the sharp point of a concealed sword stick.

"Goobleys in the attic"

'Let me be more precise. If you have a God, start talking. An opening gambit might be a humble outline of past errors and regrets. In the brief span before you follow this with sincere offers to mend your ways.'

'I really don't understand,' said Jean in frustration.

Then, from the rafters, a white, morbid figure with huge milk-white cobwebbed eyes flew down on a rope. Other shapes appeared from the floorboards like ghosts rising from the flagstones in a crypt or zombies from graves. As they did so, a chill filled the air. A stench spilled out everywhere as though someone had opened a cupboard on several cans of old beans. Jean froze like an icicle but Moonster, with an expert dodge and a lightning movement, stabbed the descending Goobley in the head with the butt of his sword stick. The Goobley, stunned in mid air, held for a second and then dropped through a gap in the beams.

The silence of the Goobleys was awful, but their pace slowed a little once the first had fallen. Jean could only see them in the dimness at the penumbra of light when they flitted beneath a skylight. The dimness made them more sinister. Jean remembered the shambling thing he had seen through the lift window some hours before.

'Sorry, 'said Moonster between his teeth. 'That jarred rather. I was trying to keep it simple. Do you recall asking what Goobleys ate?'

'Yes,' said Jean

'No one has ever reported their culinary habits but I have a suspicion that long attendance in these parts would give a definitive answer.'

'I think I understand...' said Jean.

'Are you a master of esoteric martial arts?'

'No'

'Do you possess the profound wisdom of pugilism?'

'No'

'Then, when you have nothing to fight with, run!' said Moonster.

'I can't just run,' said Jean, although he felt he could.

'I'll hold them off. You run ahead. There is a good exit to the roof three skylights off. Jump to the skylight. There is a catch. It's easily opened.'

The Goobleys had begun a slow mesmeric advance.

'What about you?'

'Go,' said Moonster. 'The drainpipe...' He whirled his sword stick into the dimness. There was a sickening sound.

'Now or never,' shouted Moonster, fanning desperately with his coloured folder.

Fear made Jean jump forward. Fear of the Goobleys, fear of the note of fear in Moonster's voice. He sprang to the next beam, was aware of a pale hand grabbing out; jumped again like a man leaping for stepping-stones. A pale face with vacant eyes stared into his. He could smell foetid breath, but even as he leapt his two hands pushed forward. There was an instant when he thought the thing had grabbed onto his arm, but it was too late, and he watched the Goobley fall backward into blackness. He leapt again. Then there was a desperate springing from beam to beam. Once, and only once, he turned. He saw, in the pool of light from the skylight, Moonster standing like a tiny doll miming combat with a pin. He heard a little voice smothered by the darkness of the attic screaming: 'Go!'

Then Jean ran. Tears streamed down his face as he looked for skylights.

These moments were the worst of all. The darkness, the shadows, the dim flickering shapes. Sometimes, smoke or mist would weave around the beams where some room below gave out noxious gases. Or there would be vague cries or name-calling from indeterminable places. And then Jean's terror mixed with shame as he searched for the skylights. Had he counted right? One and then, after what appeared like a whole weekend, a second; the third appearing not long after. He stumbled up some packing cases. His feet sank into old cardboard, from which he expected at any moment a head or hand to appear. But none did. His hands scrambled at catches. Then he heard flopping noises approaching from behind him. His hands bled from scratching at the window bolts, but finally he found their secret. He pushed upwards. Did something touch his bare leg? He never found out, because at that point he broke the skylight. The force of his body tore the rotted frame from its hinges. Jean's head and shoulders pushed through the glass like a portrait emerging from its frame. As the frame flopped out with his body onto a sloping roof Jean rolled downwards. He fell from the edge of the roof amidst the birth of a glass-splintered galaxy.

For a second he thought he saw a startled girl. Her face pressed against a passing window. Behind her a gaunt shadow.

'*Papillon!*' Jean cried. He fell like a drunken acrobat.

'Better way to die,' he thought.

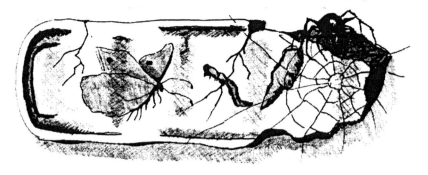

Chapter 14
The Garden

*Old Day the gardener appeared
Death himself, or Time, scythe in
hand by the sundial and freshly-dug
grave in my book of parables.*
- Denise Levertov

But Jean did not die.

Instead he rolled like a tumbler. In one instant, he saw windows and vine leaves very close up and lots of succulent grapes. (*Like Auxerre*, he thought.) In the next instant, he saw the same thing far away as though someone was putting a photograph of a scene of greenery right in front of his face and then whipping it away to reveal exactly the same scene in the distance. Then there was a jerk as his body was caught on an outgrowth of vines. He could see the guttering of the roof some thirty feet above his head, the casements of the windows and the eaves of the roof. He hung splayed out, winded for an instant and then he felt the grasp of the ivy releasing him. With his head backwards he could see briefly, upside down, the façade of the buildings opposite. Then, as the ivy boughs bent deeply under his

115

weight and his head tipped back, he saw a vast drop to an inexplicable surface like an enormous broken mirror. Jean's hands scrabbled left and right. He gripped a stout limb in his right hand. It was enough. He held on as the ivy bowed over with his weight. It swung him smack into the leaf-clad brick wall. The impact made him release his grip.

Jean began to plummet through the ivy. The heavy vines broke his fall as, with scrabbling hands, he bounced like a pinball from bough to bough. How far he travelled in this manner was impossible for him to determine. When his feet struck an immovable obstruction he was barely conscious.

Jean's hands gripped the tendrils of the vine before him. A wave of relief swept over his dimming awareness. Somehow he had reached the ground.

Perhaps the mind is able to assimilate distance and perspective in a single all encompassing vision. This was borne out by Jean's instinctive feeling that the ground had seemed further away in the brief glimpse he had caught of it as he fell off the roof.

The tendrils snapped. He fell like a man executing a backwards dive, arms spread wide, dimly conscious that he had been standing on an architrave, inexplicably peopled by a group of disinterested observers.

For the second time his body hit glass, the smash of the impact more electrifying than the pain.

Just as he was going to faint he landed on his back in the comfiest thing he had ever known. He sank, with arms outspread, into a green mossy bed.

For a while he simply lay there.

Slowly, Jean's eyes took in a strange sky seemingly composed of a broken mosaic; a sky so bizarre he had to look away.

In every other observable direction, Jean could see ivy clinging to ancient walls. Intertwining with the ivy were grape and vine. From between overhangs, ivy-draped windows appeared like hidden shrines. Rusting drainpipes thrust out like old pipe cleaners. These, and the backdrop of stone walls, were covered in floating crystal wort, tinged with violet, and carp liverwort in the shape of tiny crescent moons. Other mosses and lichens with little periwinkles and tiny parasols bedecked every cornice and casement.

As Jean lay recovering his breath, he thought that if there were fairies and goblins in the world, this was the place where they would live; all the mosses, liverworts and vines could provide hats, caps and shoes, tiny swords and clothes, food bowls and drinking cups; all green, emerald green. Here, they would live in a land of green and sweet smells, of healthy damp and growing things.

Jean lay still for ages. Gradually, he became aware of the insects that occupied the air and earth. He breathed in sweet smells; the perfume of wild flowers, the dank reek of loam and bark. After a while, his body seemed to have become a living thing composed of a million independent but interconnected parts. He felt that at any time it could expand outwards and become the garden, and then after a couple of eternities perhaps the sky or even eternity itself.

Jean watched the course of the dying sun fragmenting through an unusual and inexplicable sky. He felt himself joining the sun on its interminable pathways.

As Jean lay in this kind of meditational trance, he shut his eyes and became the silence. It was a silence not filled with tension, but charged instead with innumerable tiny voices below the level of actual hearing. Each insect droned its unconscious reverie. With his inner eye, Jean was able to see the noises, like bubbles of light on a black sky canvas. He heard stars made volatile, singing through the ether of space.

Then it was as if he was being sucked into a mouth, soft and slow, like butter being swallowed by a giant. At the same time, the warmth of the air was replaced by something intangible and deeper. He opened his eyes and there before him was a man who seemed composed not of skin and bone but of pots and moss.

With a start Jean recalled Moonster's words: 'Sometimes when you try and avoid a thing, you find that it finds you instead.' It appeared he had found the Green Man.

Like a magnet, the figure drew him into the absurdity of its composition.

It was as though someone had taken the skin off a clay model and found all the parts that the artist had tried to conceal. Thick muscles bound around hollow bones. In the midst of the giant misshapen face were two piercing eyes. These eyes, which appeared to focus with intensity on something else, stared through and beyond those of Jean. But he had no time to contemplate the eyes. A giant, gnarled hand was stretching towards him with the palm open. The other held a watering can.

He thinks I'm a plant, thought Jean. He tore his gaze from the piercing eyes to the moss bed on which he had fallen. And then to his amazement the moss appeared to change form and writing appeared. It was like one of those pictures (which Jean had always thought a con) that you see on market traders' stalls in the street, the ones where you have to look for ages until something 3D jumps out at you.

As the giant figure leaned over him, he heard the tiniest voice saying 'Who knows when he will come? Who knows whom he will take? Who knows where we will be taken?'

"The empty lifeless statues stood or lay in postures
of death or pain"

And there beside him were two snails, just hidden under the overhang of a rock. They were talking by rubbing antennae together but Jean could hear it easily in the overcharged air.

'It is all for the good,' said the larger one.

'We can but hope and revere the Gardener.'

And then beside him he heard other voices clamouring. 'This life is only a fleeting thing, a day an eternity, but over before we can take a breath. The Gardener reaps and he sows, but for us his reaping is the end of all things.'

And then the insects were everywhere, their tiny incessant voices claiming, protesting, shouting, crying. Mingled with them came a slower voice – so slow that the words appeared to form a solid wall in his mind.

'The bringer of life: The green gatherer: Being of sonorous movement, speak to us of the fleeting joy of another world. Green Man, speak with your hands.'

Much later, Jean could never truly recall this experience, but now he appeared to see and understand the words that formed in the moss around him.

And then the Gardener's hand met his and he felt himself pulled upwards, out of the succulent moss. Pulled into the folds of the thick leather-like clothes that appeared to be growing from the Gardener's solid body. For an instant, Jean thought it was Death enfolding him in impenetrable arms, but then he felt a sense of overwhelming security. For the first time since he had learned of *Papillon*'s disappearance – or maybe even the first time since his father had been taken to the terminal ward, – he felt utterly safe. What had his father said? 'Most problems are solved in an embrace.' Until now, Jean had never realised what this meant.

The Gardener carried Jean gently, as though he were a wounded bird. He transported him through the enclosed emerald spaces, the rising trellises bedecked with beautiful vines and hanging purple grapes: through the steaming, thrumming air. As he walked, every tiny creature blazed paths of stunningly brief speculation across Jean's dazzled eyes. The smell of the damp, misty, peaty clothes permeated his nostrils in a deep hum of earthy life. All around, birds fluttered upwards or nested in brooding contemplation along the walls.

And these walls, festooned with ivy and moss, led upwards, upwards in steep terraces until they reached the underpinnings of the great glass mosaic above the quadrangle. A distant frame, structured just above a row of first floor balconies and terraced pavilions, encircled the entire quadrangle. The great skeleton of a greenhouse, with a hundred thousand windows for squares, fragmented the death throes of the sun like a wild glass chessboard. The walls that led to this giant glass canvas were damp with the eyes of toads and newts that stared from cracked mortar and the spaces between broken stone.

One broken drainpipe, projecting outwards at an angle from the wall, produced a fountain of leaking water. The water burst like a rocket, buried in the ground but still firing its streaming jet; an entrenched firework that sprayed fine water in Jean's face as he passed. He saw that it had created a tiny river that ran through the garden along a chain of successive open gutters. These gutters led in turns to small pools, once artificial but now so old they appeared to have merged like ancient monuments into the natural world. In these waters, little sticklebacks and minnows nested and darted. Water spiders ran across their surfaces to be eaten by watching frogs and tiny newts poised like marvellous acrobats in and above the deep, limpid pools.

Everywhere, life threw up its hands and shouted

happily, and through it all the Gardener strode as though balanced on perfectly weighted stilts.

At intervals, the Gardener would pause. He would tuck Jean under his arm and then with his immense hands he would pull and pluck, push or play, crop and shear. Every point of his being tended to the needs of his creatures and plants. He was minister to a world.

Each time the Gardener stopped Jean could hear the tiny voices; the slow and the quick, questioning of the purpose of it all.

The Gardener never answered.

For an immeasurable time, they paced the garden. The sun filtered through the broken mosaic above and glinted from the balconies and verandas. At times, Jean felt as though he had plunged into water and was observing, from beneath, the hallucinogenic rippling of reflections in a lake. Then, as though to confirm that he had drowned, he saw apparently approaching him, a small army of shining people. They were at the far end of the garden, enshrouded by an enormous weeping willow that rose like a tasselled cape over them all.

But Jean was the one who moved. And they waited, as he was carried towards them, still and silent like administrators of a new heaven.

As he drew closer, Jean could see that they were all statues and gargoyles. Many were broken or cracked in places. Their stubbed and splintered faces stared through marble, mummified in moss. Jean recalled the bust that had spoken to him outside the library. He knew instinctively that these things would never speak. Without exception, they were broken. If ever a spirit had animated them, it had long since flown.

Here, with a deep sigh of weariness, the Gardener gently put Jean down.

He thinks I'm a statue, thought Jean. At that moment, he saw that on various parts of the surrounding walls there were a number of architraves. One architrave lay just beneath the canopy. The others were observable in varying degrees through the holes in the greenhouse glass. Statues in various stages of disintegration could be seen perched there in serried lines. Great gaps in their number were signalled by corresponding holes in the glass. From the ends of the drainpipes and at other intervals and culverts, gargoyles also rested; some above, some below the canopy. They opened their mouths, snarled, spat out or shouted in silent mockery, as though an audience of devils attended a preview of the Garden of Eden.

When they fall from the sky, Jean thought, *the Gardener puts them all here.*

The giant form of the Gardener rose, looked with distant eyes at Jean and the statues, and walked until he disappeared into the greenery, never to be seen again.

Jean felt a sense of desolation creep over him. The empty, lifeless statues stood or lay in postures of death or pain. The mosaic sky, seen through the failing greenhouse, appeared to be blackening. Some of the windows of the school began to flare with candles or gas lamps. In others, there were vague electric hums. The activity beyond the glass canopy was cold, as though it belonged to a galaxy removed in time and space.

Jean shivered and his bruises and bumps all began to hurt at once. He dared to move for the first time. Nothing happened, except the blind eyes of the statues and gargoyles stared more emphatically through their moss skins. As the light died, they appeared more and more like broken ghosts.

It was then that Jean gave a little gasp. He leapt to his feet and ran, staggering forward with tears blurring his eyes.

It was *Papillon*! Her face staring at him amidst the

statues. He ran through the shapes, pushed aside some of the smaller statues so that they fell, some shattering. Then he was facing his sister.

But it was not she.

It was a statue just below life-size, an exact replica. Clearly fashioned by some master artist from a living model.

Jean wept for so long that his tears, unable to will the statue to life, seemed to drown the fading sun. The moon rose in the sky, like a hole in a stage curtain. Jean stood contemplating every detail of the figure, which had somehow become more lifelike in the moonlight. He saw eventually that it was very old; old enough for moss to gather in every fold, and for parts of the extremities to have crumbled away.

At times, a cloud shrouded the moon. Its interrupted light shone through the shattered panes above, and movements in the vine played on the face of the statue. They made it appear as though it might speak. But it did not.

'How could *Papillon* be *here?*' thought Jean. He touched the statue but it was only cold marble. With final resignation, he gave up clinging to the desperate belief that he could reanimate the cold marble.

At that point of release, he contemplated the statue again. It was the image of his sister, naked and winged, with eyes that looked up. With one hand it pointed to the mosaiced sky, while the other held a book. The base of the statue was buried in moss and Jean cleared it away to reveal some engraved words

'*Papillon,*' it said.

Papillon, *mariposa, butterfly. That must explain the wings,* Jean thought *but why not 'Michelle?'* And now it was dark. At least, the shadows were dark; the moon made everything else pale, beautiful and eerily disturbing.

Jean had never felt more alone. What could he do now? Was he trapped here forever? The garden was a beautiful place, but would he become like one of the statues? Would he be locked forever in some hideous posture or left to stare at the untouchable beauty of the garden? Was that what had happened to his sister? He fought back the tears and resolved then and there to escape. But how?

And then a leaf fell from above him and he looked up. His eyes followed the pointing finger of his sister's statue. There, way up but below the architrave, and obscured by the trunk and leaves of a vast weeping willow, he could see the underside of a glass balcony. Jean looked back to his sister's face. Her eyes were upturned. Perhaps this was the way. Maybe she was helping him now. Or somehow, he could not think how, she had known that he was going to pass this way.

Jean saw the drainpipe behind her. On it were riveted some metal bars where someone had tried to make climbing easier. He glanced at the weeping willow, establishing that it was not possible to scale it, and then he took one last longing look at the statue of his sister.

Just as Jean was about to test the first metal strut, he noticed again the book in *Papillon's* hands. He presumed it was marble like the rest of the statue but a flickering zephyr had moved one of the pages. *That shouldn't happen,* Jean thought, *in a stone book.*

He looked a little closer, and saw that the pages of the book were not stone. Or at least the first page was paper, and on it was inscribed a childlike writing. The writing had faded so much that he could not tell if it was his sister's. But Jean could read what was written:

From a window, the garden is difficult to see. Some never see it.

Jean was disappointed. He had hoped there might be something personal. For a while he found himself thinking of Mr Kay, his Geography teacher. He remembered the disturbing human look in his eyes before Jean had been sent to the stockroom. For a second, he even wished that Mr Kay were beside him, ready to give him a hand up. But then he came back to himself.

He was alone.

He looked upwards, to where the first floor balcony appeared like a chimera below the fragmented windows of the greenhouse. The old weeping willow had forced its way through the panes of the greenhouse roof just above the balcony. There must be a window somewhere up there, but it was impossible to see at this angle, in the poor light. Jean sighed and turned back to the drainpipe.

Grasping it with one hand , and then the other, Jean began to climb.

The struts helped him, but at times they appeared to threaten him like swords. His mouth felt dry and his limbs were stiff and tight. His hands in particular had picked up cuts and bruises from all the previous excitement, and his right arm, which he had hurt falling into the Head's classroom, appeared to belong to a different person.

He was quite high when he found himself looking into the open mouth of a hideous gargoyle. Its eyes appeared to stare back at him. He was not frightened until it spat. He dodged his head out of the way and the thing lunged its neck forward and tried to bite him. With one hand, Jean clung to the pipe, one foot hanging in the air, the other on a strut. He thumped the gargoyle on the nose and hurt his fist in the process. That appeared to quieten the gargoyle and gave Jean time to climb a little further. It still bit his leg as he shuffled higher, and he shook it off with difficulty.

Then, feeling like some amphibian making its first steps on land, he found that he was staring at the great arched chessboard of the greenhouse canopy. This fragile surface, starclad under moonlight, rose around him like the swell of a gigantic ocean-deep wave beating on an old harbour wall.

Slowly, like an astronaut making his first tentative disembarkation, his head and body emerged into the glinting glass-scape of a New World.

For a while he paused, trembling in the sudden cold. All around the gaunt walls rose like the amphitheatre of an enormous watching prison. Jean had his opening chance to contemplate whether the widows with lights were more worrying than those without.

Looking into the eerie moonlight, he could see overhead that there was one more gargoyle on the pipe. Just above the gargoyle was the bottom of the glass balcony. Jean saw the underside of a boot heel in the centre of the balcony, as well as tables and chairs occupied by seated figures. The whole tableau was distorted like a surrealist artwork through being upside down.

Jean edged nearer to the next gargoyle. His feet and legs ached with the strain. Some of the smaller vine tendrils were tangled up in his hair and hands. He felt suddenly weary. His breath wheezed through his throat as drew close to the gargoyle. It sported a hideously ugly face with disturbed large eyes and a tiny nose. Crustaceans of rust grew from every one of its repulsive orifices. Jean had already drawn his fist back for the first punch. He clenched his bloodied knuckles and felt his face go all tight like his hands. But then the gargoyle smiled. Jean knew instantly that it was not going to hit him or bite him. With a sudden feeling of warmth he

127

placed his hand on its head.

'Can you talk?' he said.

The gargoyle did not reply. It only smiled wider in an ugly way.

As Jean rested his hand on its head there was a brief creaking noise and then a terrific snap. With one last bemused smile, the gargoyle fell forward and without a noise dropped into the void. As it fell, old water came spouting from the hole that its departure had created. Jean clung on desperately. The water sprayed his face and hands, nearly tipping him into the night.

Somehow, despite the pain in his right arm, Jean kept going. He pulled himself hand over hand until his head came to the underside of the balcony. He rested in a little declivity, where the pipe split into two sections like a giant boy's catapult. Here, sitting in the fork of the pipe like a garden gnome, he nursed his failing strength.

From this point, Jean could see the length of the garden. If he tipped his head downward he could vaguely discern the unearthly broken reflection of the moon, shining through the cracked panes of the greenhouse roof. The light caught the shapes in the cemetery of statues and gargoyles, hooded by the spread of the great weeping willow. Further beyond, it glistered on running water, as though the moon played hide and seek with the little brooks that ran through the garden.

The greenhouse's ceiling of broken glass frames reflected the moon and stars in a splintered parody of the blackening evening. All around, the windows of the school appeared to stare down like innumerable eyes; some shuttered and blind, some warmed with flickering candlelight or ghoulish gas, some glowing with frenetic electrical energy,.

It was an awesome sight – made unbearably worse by the white faces that sometimes appeared like flitting phantoms at the dark windows. This chiaroscuro of figures, like those in a German shadow film or a shadow puppet-show, enacted eerie dances in the well-lit rooms. Sometimes, a scream or shout would fire itself into the garden from a window, but the mossed walls of the huge quadrangle quickly absorbed all sound. Jean heard other noises: The glass-blow hoot of an owl, the call of a nightjar and from somewhere nearby the chirruping of budgies. For a few minutes, before a bank of clouds made the sky irrevocably black, a distant peacock sent its cry out into the dimming light and then the murmur of running water calmed the evening like the whisper of a gentle mother.

Jean listened to this until his eyes began to close. With a start, he nearly fell from his perch. Quickly, he drew himself up. He had gained some strength from his brief rest. It had to be enough. He latched one hand onto the pipe, and the other onto the glass roof above and hauled himself into a position where he could reach one side of the balcony. He managed to pull himself up on to the balustrade and over the top.

If there had been people on the balcony, now they had gone. There were only white iron chairs and two white tables. Lying on the floor were what looked like bowling pins, seven in a row, laid out as if for a game. Jean, exhausted by the climb and the strain of the last few hours, was not given to contemplating their purpose. He fell into a seat, tucked his coat in around himself and let his head drop towards his breast.

To his left, Jean could see another balcony above the eaves of glass, and beyond it a dwindling perspective of balconies, pavilions and terraces. To his right, he could see two red velvet curtains moving lightly in the wind. Through a gap in these curtains there came the vague sound of a tinkling piano. Its cluttered harmonies were accompanied by voices that continually broke into merry laughter. A deep smell of fragrant incense wafted out from the room.

Jean listened to the murmur of the stream and the distant sound of the piano and the laughing voices until they appeared to merge into one. Then, the voices seemed to float downstream. The pianist continued alone. The cluttered harmonies changed to a plaintive melody. Single notes staggered across the invisible keyboard like a lost and hopeless child. Quietly, Jean fell asleep.

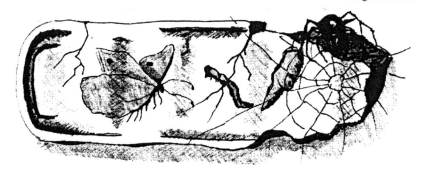

Chapter 15
The Juggler

Twit twit twit
Jug jug jug jug jug jug
So rudely forc'd.
Tereu

-T. S. Eliot

Jean awoke to the sound of a deep timbred voice. It was a melodious voice, with a lilting quality. Not friendly, as such, because it had too much pride and arrogance in it, but there were also undertones of sympathy.

Jean opened his eyes. As he was staring directly downwards, he was shocked for a second into the belief that he was floating miraculously in midair. At first, he could only see the ever-varying branches of the weeping willow. Then his vision spiralled to the distance directly beneath him. He saw the broken spout of the new waterfall he had created in his ascent. Shimmering beneath its cataract, the tiny forms of the statues and gargoyles stood in the garden below like discarded pieces in a travellers' chess set.

Jean raised his head. Directly across from him at the next table was a short powerfully-built man whose

131

frame took up the whole of a white iron chair. A crowd of older boys, clad in grey slacks, white shirts and red blazers, sat or stood around him. Then, Jean saw something inexplicable appear above the dark powerful man. Around his head a corona of spinning haloes had manifested. They scintillated in the bright air. This sight was dazzling, exotic and unreal. It melded with the song of distant birds, the beating of their wings, the murmur and splash of water, the drifting of dandelion wishes, and the steaming air of the moss garden. It seemed to Jean like something from a story: a fantasy jungle, with a troop of red-coated, English soldiers listening on the veranda to a powerful captain or preacher. Captivated as Jean was by this image, it was some time before he heard what was being said around the table, and even when he did, the words seemed to become lost in the silver halo that spiralled around the man's head.

'Speech, language, is the key,' the master was saying. 'To know something is to say it. To hear something is to know something.' His voice was beautiful, compelling. It was at odds with his eyes, which searched the crowd for listeners. In the silence a peacock called in the far reaches of the garden.

'So knowledge is a word?' asked a thin boy wearing white gloves, who stood in the powerful shadow of the man.

The English master (Jean guessed this was who he must be) did not reply. He simply carried on speaking. 'Knowledge is many words. With words, doors fall open. You can make or change things. You can re-establish existing states or invent new ones.'

'So,' said the thin boy. 'If I say "open curtains", the curtains should open.' He pointed behind him at the red curtains.

The master smiled in triumph. His eyes burned with a compelling fire.

"There was another astonished silence"

The thin boy said loudly, 'Curtains... Open!'

And they did.

Jean, however, noticed that the English master had done this, by means of a string tied to his thumb that was attached to the curtains. A waft of the strange incense perfume Jean had smelled before danced like a zephyr in the quieted air.

There was an awed silence.

Jean gave an involuntary laugh. 'That's just a cheap trick.'

Everyone turned to stare at him. The master raised his eyebrows.

Jean became uncomfortably aware that he was dressed in the crumpled muddy uniform he had worn since he arrived. Again, he had spoken without thinking, but he had to carry on. 'Look at this,' he said, and drew the chalk from his pocket. He chalked the word 'open' on the back of a chair. He turned it around, and was about to open the curtains to demonstrate how silly the previous scenario had been, when the curtains opened of their own accord.

There was another astonished silence. Jean was no less astonished than the rest of them.

After what seemed like a long time, the English master looked Jean fully in the eye and said, 'The written word is powerful, but it is only a spoken word made static. My words can make reality now; yours can only suggest it.'

'What do you mean?' asked Jean.

'The man who is master of words is master of truth.'

'I don't understand.'

'Then let me give you a problem to ponder. It is a problem that has exhausted the talents of almost the entire intelligentsia in the school.'

The master's eyes took in the entire assembly. He lifted his broad hands. 'Some say there is a garden in the school and some say not. Some say that to find the garden is to find happy rest from all cares. Have you heard this?'

'No,' said Jean, 'but I've seen the garden. So can you, if you look yourself. Look behind you.' Jean pointed. 'There it is.'

The master frowned but did not follow Jean's suggestion. Instead, he smiled smugly with a sidelong glance at his students. They all nodded like well-rehearsed puppets. 'Tell me,' said the master, 'have you ever thought you have seen something, a friend, say, approaching in the distance, only to find it was not your friend?'

Jean thought of *Papillon*. 'Yes.'

'So your eyes were deceived?'

'Yes.'

'If your eyes can be deceived once, then is it not possible they can be deceived many times?'

'It's possible.'

'So if I look behind me...' the English master smiled. 'I should see a garden yet my eyes might be deceived.'

'True.'

'Then I cannot know I have seen a garden, therefore I cannot know if it is there.'

'But you can hear the birds, smell the moss...'

'If one sense fails me, why not the others? The garden, as doubtless you understand now, cannot be known by the method you suggest. It remains only an illusion.'

The boys nodded in approval and the master opened his arms wide in a big gesture.

'Words, even as I speak, are the master and the way to reality and knowledge.'

The master talked on, and Jean lapsed into sulky silence. Visions of his father lying ill in a hospital bed appeared in his mind. His father loved books and he had always said that the written word was one of the greatest gifts. Jean had an idea. Even while the master continued to lecture his students, Jean climbed up onto the table, and cleared a space in the ivied wall above it with his hands. Here, he wrote in large letters

WHEN YOU ARE GONE

WHERE WILL YOUR WORDS GO?

For some time, the master ignored what Jean had done and continued to lecture in his compelling voice. Then he appeared to notice the writing for the first time. He stopped and stared down at it, waiting until he had all the students turned to look at Jean's message. When he spoke, it was with great feeling.

'They will be left in the hearts of those who have heard,' he said simply.

'But as long as you live,' said Jean, 'and those who have heard still live, they can see my words, and those who come after will see them as well.'

The boys looked at the words. The master looked at Jean.

'Maybe,' said the master. 'But my words can change things *now*! The lesson is over. The existence of a garden is mere hypothesis. It is a weak hypothesis, based on emotion, on the ephemera of the senses. There is no garden.'

Jean stared at the English master in dumbfoundment. He looked to the boys to see if they had fallen for such obvious absurdity.

None of them acknowledged him. They picked up their books and pens and began to disappear through the curtains. Last to leave was the master. He rose up with heavy dignity, then wrapped his black cape around his sturdy frame and walked past Jean without even glancing at him, into the room beyond.

Once everyone had gone, Jean realised what the silver halo had been.

A short distance away on a tiny circular platform level with the balcony a tall blond boy clad in grey trousers and white shirt was standing on one leg, juggling seven silver hoops. To watch the ceaseless movement of his elbows and the graceful turn as his hands fed the hoops was like observing the perfect mechanism of an old fashioned watch. For some time Jean stared as the boy sent the hoops wherever he wished. He caught them on his back, rolled them down his arms, changed legs, flicked them all up in the air and began to cascade them between his hands like shuffling a pack of cards. All the while his sinuous body weaved a peculiar snake-like motion in balance with the very air. Finally, the boy shook his long hair, placed both feet on the ground and leaned back slightly. Jean thought he was about to fall but instead he pushed his right arm behind his back, cupped the hoops and sent them through his legs with his left hand only to catch them with his right.

With a dancer's elegance he flourished his left hand upwards and allowed the hoops to drop on to his right arm where they formed a series of arm bracelets. With that he smiled broadly and leapt forward.

Jean made an involuntary movement. In that instant he thought the boy had simply gone mad and had elected to jump to his death. Instead, by some apparent miracle, he remained poised in the air between the platform and the balcony.

It was then Jean saw the tightrope. Even so, he gulped when he looked at the distance between it and the greenhouse far below.

'I believe you!' the boy shouted. He grinned and took a pace forward.

'What?' Jean shouted back.

'About the garden. I believe you, not him.'

'Thanks,' said Jean. He moved to the edge of balcony. 'How do you manage to do that; the juggling, I mean?'

The boy turned a somersault and landed a hair's breadth from the balustrade of the balcony.

'I get a lot of practice,' he said, smiling. Jean could see that the boy was a little older than himself. His pale blue eyes held a palpable innocence, a meld of wonder and enthusiasm. 'You see I believe the garden is there and *he* doesn't like it. So, as a punishment, first he made me stand here. Then he made me juggle with a single ball, then two, then three, until I got to seven. Then he changed the balls to hoops. Then he made me stand on one leg. It's all a punishment, but he doesn't know that I enjoy it all. Even now, when he's gone and has forgotten me, I'll go and juggle all day and night. When he tells me to juggle on no legs, I will have learned to fly, and then...'

'Why can't they see the garden?' Jean asked abruptly

'You can actually *see* it?' With each reference to juggling the boy had produced a hoop. Now he walked along the rope towards Jean. The circle wheel of the flying hoops gave the illusion that the hoops themselves, like some vast propeller, were suspending him in the air.

Jean shrugged. 'All you have to do is look down.'

The boy laughed. 'Don't you know that you can never look down from a tightrope?'

'Well, why not look out from one of the windows? Surely someone can do that. I see faces appearing in them all the time. Someone could look.'

'But they never do,' said the juggler. 'Windows are only for letting in light and keeping cold out.'

'You can look through them too.'

'Maybe you can,' said the boy. He had reached the balcony now and his pale calm eyes stared at Jean, as though he could look right through him. 'Some gardens are there even if you can't see them,' he said wistfully. 'I believe it.'

'Grimshaw!' came a voice from within. 'You can put these hoops down.' The thin boy looked out from between the curtains. 'The messenger has arrived with some news we should all hear.'

Expertly, Grimshaw caught all the hoops in one hand. He smiled at Jean. 'I believe,' he said and then ran through the curtains.

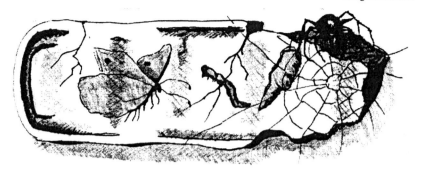

Chapter 16
One Way Out

*Silence is argument carried out by
other means.*
- Ernesto `Che' Guevara

Again faint laughter sounded on the air and the sweet
perfume drifted out to the balcony. Jean looked to left
and right. Unless he learned quickly how to walk a
tightrope, the only easy way to continue his search
would be to venture through the curtains. He looked one
last time at the statues below through the glass bottom
of the balcony; he could no longer see the statue of
Papillon. Then he stole a glance at the moss garden;
sunlight pierced the many openings of broken and
splintered frames. An exotic bird darted like a flying
sweet across his vision. It vented a single hoot as it
found a well-travelled airway through gaps in the
frames. Jean contemplated the whole glittering emerald
jewel of the garden, as though to convince himself it did
really exist. For a second he wondered if it *would* simply
disappear when he turned his back on it.

Then, he pushed through the curtains into a heavier
air.

141

The room was dimly lit by tiny flickering flambeaus; but exotic tapestries bedecked the walls, deep scarlet and green. Each displayed gold-clad Eastern adventurers and princes. Huddled groups of students sat or reclined on cushions as incense smoke wafted lazily through the air. Their red blazers merged with the deep hues of the tapestries so that at times their faces seemed to be part of the tapestry. Among the reclining and seated figures, half-naked boys wearing turbans stroked the air with lazy palm fronds. In a far corner stood a piano with a man slumped over the keys.

Discussions stirred from each of the huddled groups. Their animated gestures reminded Jean of the movements of the tiny puppets in a paper theatre set he had once owned. He remembered the excitement of that as well; the possibilities of things about to happen, the air of exoticism and unreality.

The thin boy began to speak in a low voice, charged with feeling. 'It's as absurd as attempting the fastest motion,' he said. 'Just say we employ a tiny juggler, about the size of Grimshaw's hand, and he spins a little Diablo very fast. Would we then believe that a slightly bigger juggler employing a slightly bigger Diablo will achieve a greater speed? If you were a nail pinned to the rim of the Diablo... No, Pensive, I'm not saying you are a nail...'

The heated talk faded into the sea of voices. Jean let it spill over him and began to take in the details of the room.

The English master was seated at the far end below a small podium. Near to him were the thin boy and the juggler, whose hoops glinted in the dim light of candles placed at intervals on small tables and in alcoves. From these alcoves, exotic statues stared between the tapestries, frozen in lithe dance postures. Acrobats, gods and strange demons glowered like the silent audience of a gladiatorial contest, some so still and mute that they resembled mummified bodies in a South American burial cave. Others possessed so much internal activity they appeared about to leap into the room.

Jean sat down on a cushion and one of the half-naked boys offered him a cup of tea. 'Lotus blossom?' enquired the boy, grinning to show very white teeth, 'or Tiger Chai?'

'Lotus,' said Jean. He had no idea what either tasted like, so supposed it did not matter which he chose. 'Is this English?' he asked

'Oh, yes,' said the boy, pouring tea into a tiny cup. 'It's always English. At least it has always *been* English But there has been talk of change. The new English master is keen on change.'

Jean could hear the master talking to the next group of students. His low but powerful voice broke through the higher pitched chatter of the boys. For a while, Jean sipped the tea and allowed the master's persuasive voice to spill over him.

'...an amalgamation is the only possibility. All this talk of a garden is mere conjecture. We must transform, transmutate. We must deal with reality. We must touch the real world with our fingers and shape it. Listen to me. Science and English together. They will supply the physical transformation of the words that we utter. We will not escape, for that is impossible. How can one escape oneself? But we will transform, transform and transmute...'

The words were like a hypnotic chant. Jean pulled his head up quickly. His temples were beating to a strange vibration. A light humming filled the air. Slowly, with a peculiar jerking movement, the pianist began to play a light glissando. It evolved into a tune that Jean recognised but could not name.

The juggler looked across to Jean and smiled at him. Then he got to his feet. He picked up his hoops one by one, flicking each up with his left foot onto his right shoulder, then rolling the hoops to his left hand. He began to juggle them. Surrounded by a mesmeric cascade of hoops, he walked over to Jean and sat down beside him. For some moments, Jean stared at the juggler's hands. They were the most beautiful hands he had ever seen; thin and elegant, with long tapering fingers. They moved constantly and the supple muscles beneath the skin rippled with feline grace. Grimshaw winked, held up his left hand, and with a deft movement pulled a pencil from his nose. Then somehow he made it disappear into thin air.

Jean smiled. 'You do tricks as well?'

'My art is deception,' said the juggler. 'I'm very good at deception.'

'How is juggling deception?'

'It deceives the air. Contrawise, slight of hand deceives the eye.'

'But it's deception for a good purpose,' said Jean.

'Sometimes I feel like an actor,' said the juggler, in a far away voice. 'The whole purpose of an actor is to make the completely artificial appear completely real.' He smiled.

'But you make the real appear artificial. You make a real pencil appear to be nothing. Magic is about entertainment, amusing people.'

The juggler sighed at the mention of magic. 'I don't think it's always the way you see it. There are darker applications.'

There was a pause, but Jean was not uncomfortable with it. Instead he breathed in the incense and listened to the low drone of voices around them. Eventually, he said, 'Do they just talk here then, or does somebody actually *write* in these English lessons?'

144

The juggler shook his head and put his fingers to his lips. Jean leaned closer to him. 'Sometimes,' the juggler whispered, 'although the English master forbids it, some of us write.' He tapped his pocket and then, with an elaborate flourish, revealed a deck of oversized cards in his hand. 'Pick a card,' he said, smiling.

Jean smiled back and chose a card. When he turned it over, he found he was staring at the King of Spades. The juggler took the card from Jean's hand, turned it, then handed it back to Jean. The King had disappeared and in his place there was some neat, flowing script. It was a poem.

White Rabbit

Tired with walking endless walking
Walking weary with the night
Where the roads and streets are silent
From light to dark and dark to light

In the morning crowds like rabbits
Shelter here in mutual sight
But for now there's only walking
From light to dark and dark to light

From light to dark and dark to light
Still a breath a pause a breath
Gent my footsteps quiet treading
Still a breath a pause a breath

At the centre of this city
Where the daylight crowds will form
In the graveyard shift grey rabbits
Take possession of the lawn

And I alone and tired of walking
Tired enough to wish respite
Watch these timid twins and gaze
From light to dark and dark to light

And I alone observe a rabbit
Mirror at the deep of night
Doomed unlike his grey covey
To tread starclad in clothes all white

Dark the tailor's foreign humour
Bright the coat that mocks the night
Lonely joy the endless walking
From light to dark and dark to light.

'But this is about Gent,' said Jean in excitement. 'That's in Belgium, next to my country. Did you write this?'

'It was given me, by a young lady,' the juggler replied, his eyes shining.

'But...' said Jean. His thoughts raced. This could surely not be his sister. The writing was too adult.

The juggler suddenly seized Jean's arm, gripping it with his slender hands. 'Some say there is a room in the school, a room where the walls are bedecked with writing, all the wisdom of the ages, all the tales untold, all the poetry of life, all thoughts unsaid. They are all in a single room, hidden in the school. They call it the Graffiti Room. I believe them. You must believe in the room if I believe in the garden.' He let go of Jean's arm, his face shining with a peculiar ecstasy.

Then the noise of a gong boomed out; a deep low vibration. The pianist continued to play. The piano's tones lightened but the repetitive melody still teased Jean with its familiarity.

The boy who had served tea announced: 'The messenger.' There was a low buzz of conversation.

146

Moonster walked into the room, sporting his black trousers, maroon velvet waistcoat, watch chain and spotted green bow tie. He held his stick with the dignity of a Roman eagle bearer. If anything, he was paler than the last time Jean had seen him, and his clothes seemed overlarge for his frame. He walked up to the English master and in a voice that Jean could only just hear said, 'The experiment failed.'

The English master's face paled but he held himself together. 'Then we must try another subject?'

'I only deliver messages; advice is best sought from your colleagues.'

'But there is so little time,' said the English master, half to himself.

Moonster shrugged. He looked across at Jean in a subdued pensive fashion. Then, with his eyes still on Jean, he said, 'Is that the message you want me to deliver?'

'No,' said the master. 'Take a message to history. Suggest an alliance. It...has to stop.'

He looks scared, Jean thought.

Moonster nodded. He walked over to where Jean was still sipping his tea. 'Thank goodness you made it,' he said. He sat down on the little cushions and rested the little message stick on his crossed legs

Jean smiled. 'I'm more pleased about your being here. I felt like a traitor deserting you.'

Moonster shrugged. 'No, it wasn't like that. I knew what I was doing. If you could have helped, genuinely helped I mean, I would have asked you. I know you would have done what was needed.'

'Thanks,' said Jean.

'I wouldn't be in a hurry to drink that tea,' said Moonster frowning. 'Tea around here is not all it appears. Have you asked Grimshaw here about your sister?'

Jean looked into his tea. The pink fragrant liquid appeared okay, but he put down the cup and turned to the juggler. 'Have you seen a little girl at all? She's about seven years old, black hair.'

'Yes, I have,' Grimshaw replied. 'The young lady we called *Papillon*. Once, I saw her. She gave me this poem.' He held up the card. 'She stood on the balcony for a little while and...'

The gong sounded again. The little tea boy stood up hurriedly. 'The Head,' he announced, his voice trembling.

A silence blanketed the whole room. The pianist stopped playing. Faces turned first to each other and then everyone turned to the English master. A look of pure panic flitted across the master's face, to be replaced by one of stern desperation.

'Oh no,' said Moonster, his face masking over with a blank expression.

Curtains opposite those to the balcony swung open wide and two enormous doors behind them opened inwards. Jean saw abject fear in the faces around him. No one moved. For a second he could hardly believe that here were people more frightened than himself. Without fully understanding why, he got to his feet. If the Head was about to walk in the room, he would face him standing. Moonster, with a surprised glance at Jean, stood up too. Then Grimshaw the juggler stood up, trembling but apparently encouraged by his companions' example. The other boys and even the master remained seated, numb with terror.

With no regard for dramatic tension, the pianist began to play once more.

Beyond the open doors, a faint chugging noise vibrated from the corridor. Mist or smoke spewed into the room. Its tendrils writhed like the searching tentacles of an amorphous octopus and to Jean they seemed to be composed partially of voices; faint, distant voices that cried, shouted, begged, or wept.

'Oh, God,' said Moonster in a hollow voice. 'It's a trick. He's not coming.'

On all sides, the boys erupted into a screaming panic. Some clutched each other, some covered their eyes. The master jumped to the podium and raised his hands, but Jean could see pure terror on his face, and then a sudden awful realisation. The master appeared about to speak, but then he fixed Jean with an amazed stare. Jean saw that the master realised, as one realises a trusted bridge has proven false, that words would do nothing.

'What is it?' shouted Jean to Moonster.

'The thing from the corridor,' said Moonster. 'The Head's sent it here.' Moonster glanced around himself quickly. The mist spilled into the room like a dismal fog rising from the sea.

'It's too late,' Moonster said

The juggler screamed.

'Run!' shouted Jean suddenly. 'Run for the garden.'

'No chance,' said Moonster. 'We'd never make it to the window and... *the garden?*' Moonster gave Jean an incredulous look. 'Is there a garden?'

The mist began to envelope the boys like an affectionate but repulsive ghost. As it gripped them, the master raised his hands higher, tried to speak, but his face convulsed in a stricken grimace and no words would come.

Grimshaw took one look at Jean. The look said a lot of things. He grinned and whispered, 'I believe.' Uttering a whoop, he leapt forward and broke through the mist, scattering his cards and spinning hoops around himself like a protective halo. Moonster looked as if he was about to try running too, but the mist was closing in, and the chugging, screeching and begging were enveloping the whole room. Through it all, the insanely melodic repetition of the pianist tinkled out on battered keys.

'Think of something else,' said Moonster. 'Quick.'

Jean sent his thoughts flying everywhere and his hands followed them. They struck the chalk. 'Use your intuition' his father had once said. Now, it was all Jean had.

He pulled the chalk from his pocket and drew a circle around Moonster and himself: Then another circle. Inside the circle, he wanted at first to put signs of the zodiac – he had seen this done in films as a protective enchantment – but didn't have enough time and could not remember all the signs, so he quickly wrote $E=MC^2$, Einstein's formula of relativity. *It has to be powerful enough to baffle any living mist,* he thought, remembering how the formula had baffled him when his father had once tried to explain it.

The mist was everywhere now; the noise. Screeching blocked out Jean's senses.

Intruding into it, like a broken music box, the pianist continued his cascading melody. Then, in the midst of the horror and confusion, Jean remembered what the composition was. It was 'The Baricades Mysterieuses,' a piece that his father had become obsessed with as the illness took him. The knowledge stabbed Jean like a knife. It conjured images of his sick father: hopelessness, grey walls, white shroud-like sheets, guttural coughing. Was that his father's voice in the mist, one of numberless screaming souls?

Jean huddled back beside Moonster, who had drawn his swordstick. He gripped it futilely with white, clenched hands.

Moonster smiled a grim, hopeless smile. 'I told you about the tea,' he said and the world shone its shoes a deep, deep black.

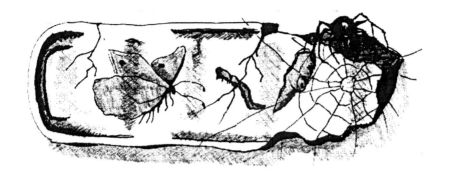

Chapter 17
The White Crow

Some are born to sweet delight
- Blake

Jean opened his eyes to find that his head was resting on something soft, which he quickly discovered was actually Moonster's chest. For a moment though, he could not think about this, but only concentrate on the horror before him.

The first thing Jean saw was what had to be the English master, who was only recognisable by his clothes. His body, mummified like an ancient Egyptian, lay against the wall, its arms spread out in a parody of the gesture he had been making before Jean had blacked out. The face was terrible in death. Jean remembered seeing a picture of a buried Egyptian King, who had been wrapped in sheepskin and interred alive. This was the same face before him, pleading with him in shocking silence.

Then, like lesser terrors, but making the whole picture more awful because of their numbers, Jean saw heaps of mangled skeletons strewn across the floor. They lay beneath a layer of fine dust, clad in rotted clothes like the fallen in some ancient war. Everywhere there was evidence of dissolution and age, except in a track of footprints impressed in the dust. These footprints led from the chalk circle to the balcony. Here, just before the curtains, the dust was disturbed by a light breeze. Strewn along the track of prints were the shining hoops of the juggler. They lay like frozen whirlpools amidst the scattered court cards.

Attending to this hopeful sign helped deflect the miserable sights around Jean. His mind was so overloaded with horrific impressions that it needed something, *anything,* optimistic to cling to. He said aloud, 'I wonder if he made it?'

'I wonder how *we* did?' said a voice beneath him. 'Would you mind removing your head from my chest?'

Jean did so.

Moonster sat up and dusted himself down. He put the cover on his swordstick.

'It must have been the circle I drew,' said Jean.

'Yes, quick thinking, guileless faith and a magic circle are sometimes all one needs.' Moonster cast a jaundiced eye around the room and visibly paled. 'Let's go now, while we still exist.' He rose slowly to his feet and gingerly stepped from the circle. Warily, he stalked across the floor to the open door. Here he paused, as Jean began to follow him.

It was like treading on tiptoe over a forest floor littered with dry branches. Bones jutted from old red blazers, as though the victims had speared themselves with their own ribs. Mouldering eye sockets stared without sight at hands without skin that reached hopelessly across the floor. Hair still clung to skulls.

Jean reached the threshold of the door, one foot poised above a broken ribcage. Moonster stared at him with an unfathomable expression. Jean's foot placed itself just beyond the ragged pile of bones. A loud report smacked from the walls. It sent dust swirling through the air and the rotting palm fans waved gently in dead hands.

The melody of 'The Baricades Mysterieuses' began mysteriously to play again. It was slower, painful in its hesitation. Jean's hands grew clammy. He felt as if the floor might break beneath his tiptoeing feet.

He turned to where the piano player sat. In the faint morning light he could see the grotesque figure had hands that did not move. Only the body lurched in a mechanical way, the grey hard lines of its wrinkled head bobbing uneasily, as though on a thread.

Moonster gave Jean a look of mild surprise. 'You didn't know?'

'No,' said Jean, lowering his foot.

'The pianola,' Moonster said finally. 'It always plays the same piece, whatever the occasion.'

The familiar corridor with the rooms, the grilles and the pools of light spread out before them. Moonster looked up and down it. 'Follow me,' he said, 'but be quick, or we'll end up like them.' He shrugged his left shoulder to indicate the remains of the English class, and then began striding off in his purposeful way, along the right hand corridor. Jean raced behind him.

Jean was glad to be out of the shocking silence of the English Classroom, but after a few minutes in the corridor he somehow felt the presence of the corridor monster. It crept up from the floor through his feet and legs like cooling water in a tepid bath.

'What happened in there?' he asked Moonster.

'Do you feel your legs?' said Moonster, not pausing for a second.

'Cold.'

'Yes. Remind you of anything?'

'It's like the feeling I got in the English Classroom just before...'

'That's why we're not waiting,' said Moonster.

They had come to a large fireplace in the corridor wall. It was guarded by a cast iron grille. But Jean was not surprised when Moonster produced a little hoop from his pocket with an enormous bunch of keys on it. Quickly selecting one, he opened the grille. 'Just close it after you,' he said and disappeared up the chimney.

Jean waited down below. His feet and legs grew colder and the creeping, freezing sensation spread throughout his whole body. He could now hear faintly, with a kind of inner ear, the distant chugging of the monster.

'Moonster!' he shouted and suddenly felt that he had been led into a trap. The grille looked like the bars of a prison and the coldness had reached his head. Where was Moonster? Had he led Jean here only to betray him?

A head popped out from behind the grille and Moonster's upside down face appeared. 'The ladder,' he hissed and pointed with one hand to the rungs inside the chimney flue that Jean had not noticed before.

With a quick leap, Jean jumped onto the rungs. He was pleased to see that the flue was unusually clean. He recalled the faces in his history class at Park Grammar - it seemed an age ago now - and he remembered more vividly these awful tales that Mr Kent had told about the little English chimney sweeps and the huge chimney systems with their narrow and dangerous flues.

'But this must be some kind of fake fireplace,' Jean thought hopefully.

As he began to climb, he heard the loud clanging of a bell. It was the familiar funereal bell, calling out the class changes as it had done doubtlessly for interminable years. Jean heard chairs scrape, and it sounded like a thousand pieces of chalk being dragged over a thousand blackboards, but he had no time to look back.

154

As Jean clambered quickly up the rungs, he could see that Moonster had turned himself back to the right way up. Now his lithe figure, mostly obscured by his pair of immaculate brogues, was upright and climbing like a monkey up the flue. Jean could also see a tiny flicker of light high above.

The chimney system was complex and defied any of Jean's attempts to unravel the mystery of how smoke had actually escaped or light descended. The ladder took many turns, and at times it was almost horizontal. There were points where there was no ladder at all, and often, which was much worse, no light. Fortunately, there were only a few sections where the chimney narrowed drastically. Here, Jean was forced to press his knees and elbows against the sides of the flue. Then, when his shoulders and elbows were firmly fixed, he shuffled his legs up. When his legs were fixed, he shuffled with his shoulders like a little 'chummy'. In these places, Jean felt acid rising in his gorge. He was well aware that he could easily get stuck, and if so there was little likelihood of ever getting unstuck.

There were times when they paused, Moonster frowning in the dim glow like a Sunday-dressed sweep. Many times they waited, listening to distant shouts or low conversations coming from fireplaces below, while Moonster made little shorthand notes on a pad. Twice they had to leap over smoke-filled chasms, holding their breath as they did so. At one juncture, Moonster took out a concealed hand-held brush and a small metal scraper. With a flourish, he removed some tar deposits left by log fire smoke. 'Getting too dirty,' Moonster said. 'Must keep up appearances.' Here the air smelled strangely sweet and for a while they watched the smoke curl upwards into unknown recesses.

It was becoming apparent to Jean that some sections of the flues were redundant while others remained in constant use. Moonster had evolved a path to avoid the working flues and Jean marvelled both at the other boy's encyclopaedic knowledge of the chimney system and his enduring immaculate appearance. Jean also quaked inside a little at the thought of what would happen if Moonster lost him. Again and again the vision of rooms full of rotting bones clambered into his thoughts.

Sometimes, despite all his efforts, it was he who lost Moonster. Moonster would shout and then, with a little irritation, two brogued feet would appear, or if there was room – and by anyone else it would have been showing off – a head.

At one point, in a horizontal shaft, Moonster darted ahead so quickly that Jean lost him altogether. There were three possible paths forward, and one down. None looked any better than the next. Jean sat on the floor and dangled his legs over the drop into the lower shaft. He waited in a dim, nebulous light whose source, which was through some obscure chink by his head, might as well have been an eclipsed moon for all its effect. All Jean could see was three dark tunnels around him and a black pit beneath.

A smell of distant cooking rose up through the abyss. Hunger clawed at Jean's belly. How long had it been since he had last eaten? He was weary too, and his limbs ached with exertion. He had just resolved to take the left tunnel when he became aware of a small peg beside the chink of light head. Jean reached out to it. One pull on the peg and the chink transformed into a familiar tiny hole that poured forth a gush of captured light. As Jean's hand caressed the peg, he was able to trace on the panel behind it the faint impression of an initial: 'M'. 'Thought so,' he said to himself. A pattern was beginning to emerge. Slowly Jean let his eye approach the hole.

156

There was nothing to see. For a while he stared until his eye was sore and then, on a whim, he placed his ear against the hole.

In a room far away a discussion was taking place.

Jean could make out three distinct voices, all young men. By some trick of acoustics, they sounded very close

'Mr McKenna, you display a susquepedality of paunch.'

'A frivolous remark, Mr Glendinning. Pass the periscope.'

'Midden has it. Pass the periscope, Midden. Not to me. To Mr Mckenna.'

There was a long pause.

'Is it still there, Mr Mckenna?'

'Oh, yes, Mr Glendinning. It's there...'

'Is it. Is it...?'

'Oh yes, Mr Glendinning. It's still watching.'

Jean became aware of a presence. He drew back from the hole to see Moonster standing impassively over him. Jean felt embarrassed, as though he had been caught reading a private diary. Without a word, Moonster turned and leapt over the black shaft. Jean followed and the voices were left to the darkness.

Moonster ran now as though time slept in the shadows. He seemed to take risks. Jean wondered if he was upset. Occasionally, Moonster stopped and looked at Jean as though assessing him.

Once he said, almost as an afterthought. 'Lunch bell. Any, buns, doughnuts: tuck of any description?'

When Jean shook his head, Moonster frowned and said, 'Well we must simply tighten our belts.' And then he was gone, like a rat in a hurry.

The journey, while it lasted, felt endless. But it stopped as suddenly and in as an alarming fashion as it had begun.

Jean saw Moonster's silhouette at the end of a long horizontal shaft. His thin body was bowed characteristically like a preying mantis. He was clearly waiting. As Jean approached, gasping for breath, Moonster turned. He gave a rare smile. 'Lucky it's not winter,' he said. 'We only had to deal with the cellar fires and the chemists. Now in winter...' He shook his head.

Jean stood holding his sides. The air here was less stifling. The vertical shaft before them was bigger than any he had yet seen. A cold air rose from below it. Somewhere in the darkness, almost inseparable from the low moan of the wind, something wept. Moonster pointed to the frame of a small doorway on the opposite wall. It was at a slightly higher elevation than the shaft on which they stood, a open-jawed exit to another of Moonster's unlikely realms.

'Don't you think that's life, Jean?' said Moonster. 'Here we are, a couple of vagabondish, ne're-do-wells, with a scurrilous past and a propensity for ill fated decisions, and what do we find?'

Jean stared at Moonster in incomprehension.

'We find that all paths lead there.' Moonster pointed to the gaping doorway.

Jean looked at the small doorway and then at the blackness of the shaft beneath it. He shivered.

'Down below, a bottomless pit. Up above, the exit.' Moonster grimaced and cracked his finger joints. 'It's easily in reach, you know. I've leapt the gap a million times.'

Suddenly the doorway seemed to have retreated a little further.

'But knowing a thing is easily in reach is vastly different from reaching it.' Moonster looked intensely into Jean's eyes, gave a whoop, walked backwards five paces and took a run and jumped.

Jean watched as Moonster's feet struck the opposite

floor. It was a perfect landing. Moonster paused like a gymnast, turned and bowed.

Jean waited. The distant weeping had stopped. There was only the moan of the wind

Moonster beckoned. 'Don't think,' he said.' Thinking never helped anyone.'

Jean took the backward paces. He made the final leap. There was a rush of air, and he was caught in Moonster's arms.

They stood and gazed at each other in faint embarrassment and then Moonster made a great flourish and a baroque wave of his hand '*Chez nous,*' he said.

They were in a small garret, high, high above the frames that covered the garden. Jean gasped in amazement. It was a small room, barely big enough for the hammock that hung from the wall, ready to be strung across the width of the room with several ropes. These hung from large iron hooks in various places some inside, some apparently from outer gantries. A small mahogany filing cabinet and a tiny matching table occupied a cramped corner. The table was lit by a beautiful paper lantern in the shape of a pair of angels' wings and was decorated with a bowl of fruit.

There was one picture on the right hand wall: a line drawing of a woman with terribly sad eyes, who looked desperately like Moonster himself. Jean knew instantly that it was the boy's mother. There was a small dedication on the picture, signed 'M'.

> *Your eyes are like the stars*
> *On the button coat of night*
> *Sequinned on my heart*
> *Buttoned up too tight*
> ***'M'***

Jean felt enormously moved by the little poem. Somehow he knew that it was the expression of immense pain, a pain he recognised in himself only too well. He drew his eyes away and did not look at Moonster. On the left wall was a cupboard with no doors, containing lots of line drawings. Jean could see a large picture and a few smaller sketches spilling out beside it. The large picture was of an immense rooftop vista of toppling chimneys, walls, slates, crumbling spires, cupolas, open windows, frowning water towers, pavilions, terraces and rotting balconies with broken balustrades.

In the second that Jean saw this picture it appeared that it had an immediate twin. A twin with one exceptional difference. This because Moonster was standing in the place where the fourth wall of the garret should be and beyond him was the actuality of the drawn rooftop vista. Moonster had his back to Jean and his arms outstretched, but it looked as though he was greeting the noonday sun, which spilled through heavy clouds. This was the only difference. The vista was there complete: not a fantastical artwork but a simple view from a window.

But what a view. Far below, encased in its courtyard of glowering walls, the immense greenhouse glittered like a gem. On each side rose the facades of the inner court walls, spotted with innumerable windows and balconies, apertures and verandas. Moonster's garret seemed to be at the pinnacle of the eastern wall of the court. The roofscape was visible to the west, north and south.

Gingerly, Jean walked towards the vacant area. He did not like heights and he was reminded terribly of his failed attempt to jump in his own school. Moonster casually threw him an apple and sat down with his legs hanging over the yawning view.

Jean, said. 'Did you draw the pictures?'

'Yes,' said Moonster. 'The etching on the wall is of my mother and all the others are of this view, because in this school it is my favourite place.' He waved his arm behind him. 'Summer residence,' he said, examining his apple.

Slowly, because it was a long way down, Jean sat down alongside Moonster. For an age he could not speak from sheer fear of the immense drop. It was one thing to leap spaces when you had to. It was another to simply invite them over for tea. Then, as he examined the immediate surroundings, Jean began to relax.

Just above his head, there was a hanging basket with some clothes in it. The basket was suspended from a clothesline. The line stretched out like the cable of a chairlift to the opposite building, descending in a great arc before becoming lost in a tree that had grown up through the cracked frames of the greenhouse roof far below. But then Jean could not look that far without feeling dizzy. It was as well that Moonster was in a talkative mood; it helped Jean get used to the gulf of open space spreading out in all directions

'I love to see the light bouncing from the frames of the greenhouse,' said Moonster. 'I call out to the Bridge to Dreams and the thirsty towers. I like to see the sun dance on the roof-top puddles, and in the water coolers, and to watch the rain spout through the gargoyles, and listen to its dancing steps on the glass. In those happy moments, I like to watch the air and space, and imagine that the accumulating raindrops are a vast applause to the universe, an explosion of clapping hands that will go on forever.'

Jean sat for some time regarding the spires of the greenhouse, which were decorated in peeling white paint. It was mostly intact, except where trees or large bushes had pushed their way through to the sun, rupturing the timber, or where falling slates and statues from the roofs and architraves had smashed panes. In all, the frame was like the ribs of an enormous whale Jean had once seen suspended in Chambers Street Museum in Edinburgh. Only now it was a beast clad in shining glass armour.

Jean noticed that Moonster, in his description, had not mentioned the garden beneath the glass. Also, his drawings, on a second inspection, appeared bizarre in some indefinable way.

Moonster took off his green bow tie and spoke again. 'The other thing I love is the rooftops. I think I was made to look above rooftops. I think I was made to fly above them. Look!' He shouted with the first genuine display of emotion that Jean had heard him express. 'Look! The White Crow!'

And there, flapping like a solitary sea bird, a huge white crow cawed loudly. It flew from somewhere behind them. In the dizzying spaces, its path wheeled below them as, impelled by some whim, it cruised over the rooftops.

'It's headed outwards.' Moonster pointed.

And then, just as the sun dipped behind a heavy black cloud, Jean caught the dazzling brilliance of sunlight on the crow's wings. Beyond the tiny speck of its outline, pale, pale mountains rose, seen by some miracle of perspective and high air.

Then for that moment Jean could only see the shining eyes of his friend staring into the space where the crow had vanished.

'One day,' said Moonster. He took a bite out of his apple.

Moonster seemed able to make tea and cake out of invisible things. At least, they appeared before Jean in a matter of moments. He and Moonster sat on the edge of the room, looking over the rooftops in the dull sky. There was a noiseless and heavy quality to the air, so that the little white cakes Moonster produced seemed extra chewy, and the sound of the boys' mashing gums and swallowing throats appeared too loud. Moonster improvised a second hammock from an old flag and some rope, and hung both his and the bricolage from the same hook, one below the other.

'The greenhouse is a half-folded chessboard with the trees as pieces,' he whispered, as the gloaming fell upon them. 'If one could only work out the next move, one would be a winner in a greater game.' He patted the hammocks and folded and tucked and sorted them for a little while.

'The rooftops are magnetic,' he continued, after he had finished his task and had sat down again. 'But you can't sit here all night, even though tempted. You have to transfer to hammocks later.'

They sat for a long time, as rain clouds gathered. The crow did not return, nor did the clouds lift, so they could not see beyond the roofs to the mountains, but two things happened that appeared significant to Jean.

First, figures, like tiny sullen ghosts or shadow puppets, appeared in the windows of the immense courtyard below them. They danced and cavorted like animated versions of the statues that lined the architraves and ledges.

Then Jean saw something that made him leap to his feet. Among the rooftops, there must have been a rope bridge strung between two large water towers. Here, for a fraction of a second, a small girl betrayed its existence. As she walked, precariously balancing over the abyss below her. Jean shouted '*Papillon*' at the top of his voice.

The cry echoed out over the space like a phantom and was lost in the overwhelming emptiness. Moonster stared with Jean at the immensity of the roofscape, his keen eyes searching. The girl did not turn. Her tiny figure disappeared, apparently into the tower.

'Maybe,' said Moonster. 'But who really knows? We cannot check now. It's getting dark,' he added grimly.

Much later, Moonster pointed to the tower beside the second turret and said. 'It's in there. My big secret. If we get a chance I will show it to you. If we get a chance.'

After this, Moonster lapsed into silence and Jean joined him. He was feeling too depressed to talk, and even the fascination of the rooftop could not eradicate his feeling of despair at the loss of his sister. Had that been her on the rope bridge? His mind and body were too weary to know or do anything.

After a time, rain began to drop and then it started to fall heavily. Soon, there was a cascade of water, as though someone had decided to flush every toilet, empty every cistern and turn on the water-sprayer in the garden of heaven all at once. The rain obscured everything. It fell like a sheet. Jean was reminded of old tales of kings hiding behind waterfalls in secret caves.

Moonster patted him on the shoulder. Their legs were getting soaked and so they both stood up. 'Never mind,' he said. 'Here's a bath you'll never forget.'

To Jean's surprise, Moonster took off all his clothes and grabbed hold of one of the ceiling ropes. With a wild whoop, he flung himself outwards from the building. For a second, Jean thought Moonster had gone mad and was attempting suicide. Moonster swung out in the rain, his thin, muscular body lit as if with innumerable magnesium sparkles as the water droplets dashed off it. He caught another rope that Jean now saw suspended from a gantry above the garret. Now with each swing, Moonster waltzed further into the abyss and then spun back into the room; and then, like the pendulum of some unbelievable clock, he swung back and forward, to and fro, in wild, ululating joy. He seemed at once both a human boy and a sparkling, amazing water creature, suspended in the biggest open-air bath in the universe.

For a few seconds, Jean could only glare at this sight, his throat dry with fear and his belly gnawing with expectation. Then, overcome with a sheer and fierce joy, he threw off his own clothes, grabbed a rope, and impelled himself out into the dizzying space. In an instant, he felt the weight of a million raindrops bouncing off his body. There was an empty shock as he spun back into the garret, and then the infinite joy of repeating it over and over again: sliding into the rain like a ghost with Moonster. It was as if they were flicking backward and forward in time. It seemed as if they maintained this hypnotic rhythm for hours. Sometimes, they would swing in tandem as though they were riding parallel rocking horses on a roundabout, sometimes they were like two halves of a weather clock, telling fair weather or foul, and then again they spun like reckless dancers around a maypole, entwining in each other's rope. Sometimes, they would cling together, spinning around and around like twin gymnasts.

Jean could not see the abyss below because of the violent rain. But there was one occasion when a sudden bolt of lightning struck a lightning rod somewhere to the west. In that instant, the whole immense arena woke up. It was as though an immense camera flashlight had suddenly revealed an ancient roman amphitheatre. But Jean felt no fear. Even when his hand slipped on the wet rope and he slid one-handed to the knot, he remained unafraid. The abyss was there, he sensed it, but the burgeoning air seemed somehow even safer than the lighted garret.

Eventually, of their own momentum, the ropes came to a standstill outside the room, and there was only the sound of the driven air. Jean and Moonster hung motionless for a while. Then Moonster dropped to the floor of the room and Jean followed him. They both laughed until their bellies ached, staring at their naked and drenched bodies until they could not even stand up. They had to lie down for a while, until Moonster managed to conquer the laughter and the exhaustion. Finally, he got to his feet. Somehow, he produced two Persian towels and then made some tea.

They climbed into the hammocks, and lay there for a long time, swinging idly like two sailors in a becalmed ship. They sipped tea and ate biscuits in the quiet of the storm.

After a while, Moonster broke the silence. 'You asked about the corridor,' he said.

'The cold,' Jean replied.

'Yes. That is the same monster that the Head allowed into English.'

'But what kind of monster is it?' asked Jean.

'Nobody quite knows. I have heard in Science they call it the temporal machine. In English, they called it Mara.' Moonster looked over his hammock and bowed his head towards Jean in his peculiar imitation of a preying mantis. He said 'My mother gave it the name "Memories".'

Jean thought for a while. 'That would make sense. It has something to do with time: all that death.' With the word 'death', both boys felt the room draw in as though the walls had taken a breath. Jean tried to direct his attention away from the dark place in his mind, but it was impossible. The biscuits tasted too dry in his mouth. Crumbs kept appearing in his hammock, like lice that made his body itch. Every time he tried to sweep the crumbs away they appeared to multiply. He saw in his minds eye the rotted clothes swathing the bodies of the dead boys in English.

166

'I believe it is a time stealer,' said Moonster eventually. 'Not made of metal parts you know, but a time stealer all the same.'

'But in some sense it is a time prison too,' said Jean. 'Did you hear the voices?'

'Yes. You always hear the voices and they do sound trapped. Trapped in a time machine of some sorts. A time machine.'

'My father was a time machine,' said Jean, listening to the rain.

'Your father?'

'Yes. I don't know why I said that really. But he would tell me stories from the past, about Auxerre and our family who lived there. We were peasants in olden times. Then wine growers. All his stories were of the past, so he must have been some kind of time machine.'

'And where is he now?'

'Dead or dying in hospital,' said Jean.

'We all have our losses,' said Moonster after a space and then, a little later. 'But the time thief in the corridor only takes people to the future.'

Slowly, their talk faded. The gaps of silence increased as the sentences diminished like the slow fall of the relenting rain.

'Maybe we are all time machines,' said Jean.

The rain ceased. The moon came out, with tins full of white, grey and black paint. He emulsioned the world and the boys slept.

167

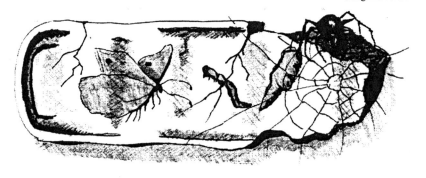

Chapter 18
The Game

*Never interrupt your enemy when he
is making a mistake.*
- Napoleon Bonaparte

*The mistakes are all waiting to be
made.*
- Chessmaster Savielly
Grigorievitch Tartakower
(on the game's opening position)

In the morning, a host of birds gathered to see them off.
Black crows, starlings, pigeons, house sparrows, and
even some sea birds, settled on the sloping roof above
and around the garret. The birds fell out with each
other. The big crows annoyed everyone, but some of the
land birds hated the sea birds, and the latter tried to
keep at a distance. They cawed and boasted, and
gathered around the hanging clothesbasket with motives
as disharmonious as their voices.

When, a little earlier, Moonster had explained that, as
well as holding clothes, the basket was used to traverse
the enormous gulf between the West and East buildings,

Jean had thought it a joke. But now, sitting in the basket, staring at the immense space around him, he was reminded of the facial expression in a newspaper article of his uncle, just before he had abseiled down a large building for charity. The face, although smiling, had expressed pure, abject hopelessness.

That was how he felt.

'Are you ready?' asked Moonster from below.

'Yes. When are you getting on?'

'Next,' said Moonster. 'The basket can barely hold the weight of one, never mind two.' He let go the rope from the hook. The birds cawed a raucous farewell.

Travelling in the basket was a difficult sensation for Jean to describe – like being flung around in a circle by a strange man, gliding down a funfair slide that suddenly has a glass bottom, or being blindfolded, taken to a funhouse, removing the blindfold to find that you have been tricked into the House of Horror.

Jean screamed all the long way down.

Below him, in the brief exhilaration of the moment, he could see the huge battered greenhouse racing upwards. His imagination had preceded his body and had already sent him crashing through the panes to a fragmented death. Instead, his progress began to slow; a window approached. The rope appeared to lead there. Was the window shut?

No, it was open. With a slow, graceful slide, Jean came to a halt in the frame of the window. It was just an opening really. There were no windowpanes and it was easy to get out of the basket and stand on the casement, which was only one floor above the greenhouse roof. It was easy to watch the basket begin to wind back towards Moonster's tiny, tiny figure way up high on the farther side.

Sunlight spilled into a small storeroom with little decoration. In the corner was a desk, and above the desk a bed, which folded into the wall. All the signs of Moonster's occupation were there: tiny origami sculptures scattered on the desk, mirrors, sticks, buns and the other things which he used to negotiate the school.

Jean heard some voices behind the door on the far side of the room. The bell rang. He could hear the slow clanging echoing through unseen rooms and the shuffle of distant chairs. With his ear pressed to the door before him, it appeared that there was little if any movement in the next room. After a while, he opened the door and walked in.

It was not empty.

They were playing chess: a room full of older boys all painfully similar to the ones who had died in the English classroom. Jean had a quick look around, but he could not see Grimshaw the Juggler. "Maybe they swap subjects here and maybe I'll catch him later if he got away," he thought.

At the far desk, a master sat with lowered head. On the walls were what Jean first took for portraits, but on a second glance he realised they were life-sized sculpted heads of boys. Presumably from Art or... He got an uneasy feeling.

The master raised his head and looked Jean up and down. He had oily black hair, swept back off his face. He produced a benign smile. There was a glint of devilment in the eyes.

'Which classroom is this?' asked Jean quietly.

'Games, of course,' said the master. 'If you had *read* the pupils' bulletin,' he continued with heavy sarcasm, 'you would be aware that this is the final day of the annual school chess competition. I assume you have come to play?'

'Yes,' said Jean. He had to have some reason for being

there.

'Enter your name on the board, then.'

Jean looked around quickly. Under the sculpted heads next to the door was a board. It was some kind of league table. But it was peculiar in that it did not have an end to it. Names had been added on little slips, one after the other, his presumably being the last, but the first and early ones were clearly incredibly old. They were written in a flowing script that even the most ignorant boy had appeared to have been able to master in olden times. There was room for more. Jean added his name to the bottom and the master smiled and spent some moments filling in a little card, which he placed in a pocket on the board specially made for that purpose. Jean's name was now at the foot of the row of pockets. The master smiled again and directed him to a seat in the far corner of the room.

There was a board with magnificent large pieces that were like statues of white and black marble. The board was level, made of leather with cream and brown squares, edged in dark black wood. The desks were oak and held a sense of great age. The room had a similar feel as that of the Head's. Time itself, by some strange paradox, seemed to seep upward from its floorboards.

Jean looked around the room. All the boys were lost in rapt attention, their pale faces tense and anxious. Some tapped nervously on the desk with long fingers. Only one boy in the far corner appeared comfortable, gloating with a fierce smile directed at his opponent, whose face Jean could not see.

There was complete silence in the room, so that when the words 'checkmate' struck the air, Jean felt them almost as a physical blow. The words came from the gloating boy. He sat in triumph; his eyes alight with sensual joy. The other boy stood up with slumped shoulders. He shook hands with the seated boy, who

172

remained as though enthroned. For a second, Jean saw the loser's terrified face. 'Don't forget to chalk it up, Aden,' said the seated boy in a quiet whisper.

'I won't, Jukian.' The loser walked over to the board with a deathly lassitude and then moved his name from second bottom to beneath Jean's. The look on his face was dreadful. The master walked over with a jovial smile. 'Any more defeats and your head will be next year's croquet ball, Aden. You better shape up your middle game. See you at Lunch, no doubt?'

Aden nodded weakly and left through the far door.

The master waved Jean over, but at that moment Moonster appeared in the classroom. He saw Jean at the game boards and he frowned. He walked up to the master and said in an intimate voice, which could still be heard in the hush of the room, 'I must take this new boy to History, Mr Huntley.'

'Yes, but he has entered his name and must play. It is the game of kings. No boy can enter the arena without testing his wits. Jukian will play him.'

Moonster quickly walked to Jean. 'The basket got caught,' he said and then he looked at the gloating figure of Jukian 'I don't know why you got involved here,' he said in a whisper. 'But it wasn't very wise.'

'It's only a game. I'm good at chess.'

'Only a game,' sighed Moonster. 'I suppose you think that life is only a game. The loser of the game enters another game, Jean. Didn't you see the heads?'

That awful feeling came over him. They were stuffed heads. He had known it all along.

'Do I lose my head if I lose?' he said.

'It's a bit complicated, but if you come to the bottom of the league table you enter a second game. It's a kind of hunt on the playing fields with you as the quarry. It's not…pleasant. Nobody has managed to come anything

173

but second in the quarry team.'

'But if it's a league...'

'Most of the boys spend every free moment coming to the room, if possible. They are addicts to it – you see, it's a bizarre league. It only goes on points gained.'

'You mean if I lose one game...'

'Your total will be zero and you will be bottom of the league.'

'But that's not fair. What about the boys who lost a lot of games?'

'At least they tried, and in the view of the Games master they also might have won or drawn a lot of games.' Moonster shrugged. 'None of this would have much significance if it wasn't the final day of the league.'

'You mean if I lose, I lose the entire league?'

'I'm afraid so. Your timing is remarkable.'

Jean blanched and looked around the room. He glanced at the grotesque heads on the wall and then as quickly looked away with the bile rising in his stomach. His eyes caught those of the triumphant Jukian. He had ordered the pieces on the board and was looking at them like a dungeon master inspecting scenarios. He looked omnipotent.

'Is he good?' asked Jean.

'He has never lost, but he isn't good,' said Moonster with a sigh. 'And he stays here permanently because he enjoys the thrill of victory. It's all he does'

'Is there nothing I can do?'

'In a games room you can only play,' said Moonster.

Jean gulped and looked at the space between him and the seated boy. He recalled a description in *War and Peace* that his father had always liked to relate. It described the no-mans' land between two opposing armies. The men in the armies did not really want to fight each other. They only advanced to discover the meaning of the gap in between. In some way he felt like this, as though he were terrified on the one hand and yet curious on the other. A little bit of him, but it was only a small bit, wanted to walk into the space and see what would happen.

Jean paused for a second and then, as though an order had been given, he gave Moonster one determined look and strode confidently to the board, sitting down on the vacant chair opposing Jukian.

Jukian remained seated. Jean held out his hand. Jukian held out his. The grip was hard. Jukian took a white and black pawn from the board and secreted them in his left and right hand. He held out both hands, barely concealing the large pieces.

'Black,' he said when Jean chose the left hand. He smiled and adjusted the pieces. As white always started the game, Jukian already had an advantage. For a good player, the chance to commence the game was everything. For a master, it was the only position from which he could be expected to have a chance of winning. Jukian pointed to the twin clocks. 'Forty-five minutes for the first twenty moves. Twenty minutes for...'

'I know the rules,' said Jean curtly.

'Chess is a game of psychology' his father had once said, 'not a game of positions'.

There were two pads for notation. Jean noted that it was old style, where the squares were named according to the piece that dominated them.

Pawn to king four was the first move, and in a flurry of subsequent movements they played the first seven moves of the Sicilian defence. It had taken three seconds and each had banged the clock down emphatically to mark the moves.

As Jukian viewed the position, Jean looked at the pieces themselves.

"Jukian's smile was only on his face"

The pawns were beautifully carved. They depicted pupils of the school in the same archaic uniform. The rooks were large water towers, each with an old fashioned aeroplane in the tower. The aeroplane seemed about to spill out. The knights were shaped like crows with small boys on their backs, and the bishops were all masters with flowing cloaks. In the centre, the king was so like the gardener that Jean almost expected it to move itself, and Jukian's queen was an incredible woman whose face had been replaced by a skull. The queen in particular was a threatening piece. Jean could only see the backs of his own pieces but he assumed that apart from the colour they were the same.

Jukian moved his bishop out.

Now, at this point, they had both followed book moves to the dot, but Jean knew that unless you were incredibly skilled or had done a lot of preparatory work, you would have to start really thinking now. Jean could already tell by Jukian's play that he knew the opening game very well. By his whole 'stance' he would be a good if not great player. But the magic of chess is that if you can do the first moves by rote, your opponent has no idea how good you really are. For all Jukian could tell from this formal position, Jean might as well be a grandmaster or simply a sound club player.

They were now beyond those first learned positions and entering that mystery land where the moves are all based on thinking ahead and reading your opponent's intentions. Jean could tell that Jukian was an attacking player, and that he was accustomed to winning. Logically, everyone must defend against him.

So, Jean began to attack.

In the Sicilian defence, the object is to hold the right of centre. Despite the name, it is an attacking opening, but it is not a wild attack. It is a steady march, fighting over one pawn: as one pawn and a good position are all a really accomplished player needs to win a game.

Jukian began to get interested in the game. He slowly fingered his lips and with a look of intense expectation began to open out in the middle game. The clock ticked on and the game began to grow like a living thing. If a player knew enough about the game, he could keep it going by creating a sound structure, by careful defence. In part, this is what Jean did. Jean only tried to calculate a few moves in advance. He had long since learned to rely on his intuition. He formed patterns in his head and placed the pieces in the pattern. Not some sequence of possible moves, but the pattern in the here and now. Did it look strong and symmetrical? Were there any obvious weaknesses? He was like a jazz trumpeter in a blues band, knowing good structures, sticking to them and just occasionally letting out a little riff of invention.

Jukian did not like it, and slowly, as games around them finished, a crowd gathered. As soon this happened, Jean knew he had won a little victory because he could sense that all the other occupants of the room wanted him to win – except Mr Huntley, who glowered from behind Jukian's head and surveyed the board with a highly critical eye. But even the Games master hovered around the board, looking at the position and muttering under his breath.

It was then that Jean discovered a new and unexpected silence. It was a silence filled with fiendish anticipation. The silence of the hunter.

Time on the clocks began to run down. Both players made a quick breathless flurry of moves. Everything tipped into the one box and jumbled around, hands flew to pieces, and only after the flurry could both consider writing down the eight moves that had just occurred.

At this point Jukian smiled, and Jean felt a hole open where his soul was supposed to rest. Because in the flurry he had placed his queen *En Prise*. (That is his queen was undefended.) As the queen is the most powerful piece on the board, all that Jukian had to do was take it and he would easily win.

And this is where the mind came in. Jukian's smile was only on his face. In his eyes, there was a mixture of fear and elation. For a chess player, particularly one who is used to winning, defeat is a terrible thing. To win gloriously is best, checkmating in an elegant or unusual combination of moves, to win is second, to draw against a good player is acceptable, but to lose is to find a chink in your armour that others would like to widen. In Jukian's face, this fear and elation expressed both the terrible fear of defeat and paradoxically the joy of prospective victory.

The question in Jukian's mind was quite simply this: Why had Jean, this unknown player who was obviously fairly accomplished, left his queen 'hanging'? Why was his best piece in a place where it could simply be removed at no obvious cost to Jukian? Why had he apparently given the game away?

This was why Jukian's eyes looked to the board and then to the eyes of Jean. On the board he could see the objective truth: The real position of events, but in his opponent's eyes...? Only there could he read the subjective truth, the motivation behind the action, and this was the bit that Jean had mastered. With poker-faced vacancy, Jean's eyes reflected the possibility that the move was only *apparently* bad.

Jukian looked again at the board and again at Jean. Was it a masterstroke – had Jean given up his queen as a sacrifice in order to make an assault on Jukian's king? Was it a trap? Or was it a mistake?

In Jean's eyes he could read nothing. Jean was looking at the board. Jean then finished his notation of the move in a way that suggested he knew exactly what was going to happen next. He let his hand hover over the column of writing to note Jukian's next move. He knew what Jukian was going to do next!

So Jukian, winner of everything in the past, tottered in the now. He said in a tone of voice that no one living had heard before, 'I offer you a draw.'

The whole crowd broke into excited whispers that quickly died as they waited for an answer. In that moment, Jukian's eyes searched those of his opponent. Jukian had backed down, but was it the right decision? And then came a reply that told Jukian that he had lost.

'Oh I don't think so,' said Jean and he stared straight through into Jukian's heart.

Jukian was clearly shocked. His vision staggered over the board, looking now no longer at capturing the queen but instead at defending his position. He made a poor move, and all the while Jean thought of his Dad in his mind and tried to look ahead.

'I am the best player in the school,' said Jukian, so quietly that only Jean heard.

'Are you?' said Jean, in a voice that dismissed best players in the school to failed probationers in a childrens' nursery.

In five moves, Jukian was staring in disbelief at the tiny crumbling landscape of his game.

With a shaking hand, he toppled his king over. 'I resign,' he said and slowly got to his feet. He held his hand out and Jean shook it.

'Move 17?' he asked, against all etiquette. 'Your queen?'

Jean picked up the queen. Now, for the first time, he looked at it as his opponent would see it. He had assumed it was the same as the other white queen but it was a statue, a miniature statue of his sister. He held the queen in his hand for a long time.

'My queen has a mind of her own,' Jean replied and got up. The crowd looked at him aghast. Some smiled, but most simply stared.

'Now,' said Moonster.' Time to go.' He took Jean by the shoulder, nodded to Master Huntley, and together they walked through the room. The boys were standing still like giant chess pieces. They stared at Jean for the length of the room. As he went through the door, a roar of applause followed him all the way down the corridor.

'Now you've done it,' said Moonster.

The corridor before them, with its puddles of light and its old green carpet, was in no wise different from the corridors of the west wing except for the change of colour.

'Done what?' asked Jean.

'Everyone will talk about your victory over Jukian. He was a great player.' Moonster gave Jean an appraising glance. 'But I suppose, like any king, there comes a time when you topple.'

Jean was elated with his success. He felt his heart soar. The storm was over. The supercharged air was full of ozone. Even here, in the depths of the old school, Jean could feel the changes. And he felt somehow that he was nearer his sister than he had ever been before. Or maybe she was nearer him. 'Where to now?' he asked happily.

'History,' replied Moonster, and they stood before a door. 'Where more kings topple than on any chessboard.'

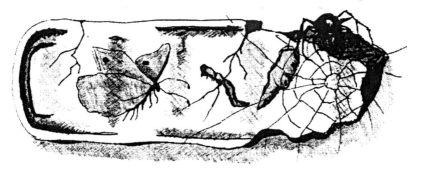

Chapter 19
A Lessin in History

*I have but one lamp by which my feet
are guided, and that is the lamp of
experience. I know no way of judging
of the future but by the past.*
- Edward Gibbon

*We learn from history that we learn
nothing from history.*
- George Bernard Shaw

On first inspection of his surroundings, Jean thought he
had stumbled in on an Art class. Everywhere he looked
he could see groups of younger children working
industriously around tables. On every table there were
tiny paper theatres, or tiny lightweight tin toys. Each
table was crowded with paper figures on sticks,
cardboard theatres of increasing complexity, or tin
soldiers and tin aeroplanes, weather balloons, horses,
knights, tables, houses, castles and clouds, elves and
fairies.

"And then there were the paper theatres"

There was a constant high-pitched chatter. Little hands moved everywhere; little figures ran and skipped between groups of pupils bunched around work tables. The pupils were around the same age as Michelle. Jean felt a pang of misery tinged with hope. Perhaps she was here

Seated at a desk behind all this crowd was a huge lady. Her hair was piled high upon her head. Her chubby face made her small spectacles appear like two coins in the circular bowl of a fountain. A flounced crinoline dress was a stage curtain for a sweep of pink bosom. She was knitting with fat nimble fingers, glancing around the room occasionally from beneath her spectacles. At times, she shouted the childrens' names in a hoarse voice.

Jean noticed that all the pupils were girls. They were the first girls, with the exception of the 'phantom' *Papillon,* that he had seen since his arrival. With that realisation, he felt the rise of hope. He saw the whole montage of the classroom as a wonderful, brightly coloured garden, alive on a summer's day with vibrant colours. Insects and butterflies, bees and bright, small birds seemed to erupt from every corner like participants in a grand festival. This image, although only a fantasy, persisted in his mind long after he had left the room. Almost in a trance, Jean walked between the tables. Conversations spilled like brooks and waterfalls all around him.

Most fascinating was the quick, expert movement of the girls' hands. With little nails like seashells and short fingers like chubby sea creatures in a lagoon their hands fluttered and darted; sewing, pasting, sticking and removing. The hands were alive in themselves. They had their own minds and the minds were quick and intelligent. Then there were the girls' voices, like swift tropical fish lighting up the room in flashes and explosions, gaily-coloured streamers, expressions of thought darting through space. Last but not least Jean found pleasure in their faces, which appeared equally pretty, like the cherubs one would find in a Raphael, yet somehow anonymous as though they were all members of the same family.

All the while Jean tried to look at their faces to see if *Papillon* was among them, but his mind was so distracted by their voices and the wonderful toys they made that he felt it would be impossible to find her. A few times he stopped, astounded by the complexity of the constructions. The first time this occurred he stood before an elaborate theatre.

It consisted of a huge ivy-strewn castle, ruined in parts. In those parts where it was sound, knights clad in bright armour were poised. They held their swords point down and stared over the battlements at a host of gnarled creatures, a little like goblins but with long legs and fearful weapons; tridents, nets and flaming spears. These sinister creatures were all advancing through the ruined sections to the remaining positions of strength. At the very summit of the castle – the keep – a tiny face stared out, and Jean could not help thinking that it was *Papillon*. But such was the activity of the young girls, placing models here and there and touching up paint and glue everywhere, Jean could not get near enough to see. The whole construction appeared to be made of wood, with its creatures modelled in unpainted clay and its knights painted gold, silver and red.

All the faces were pale and wan. The eyes glinted like metal.

And then there were the theatres of paper. Huge towering structures, in variegated colours, formed vast backdrops, where figures from Arabian landscapes flew

186

on broomsticks or Persian carpets across cardboard stages with canvas painted skies. Black bearded villains pursued women in silken pyjamas, with glass beads for gold, diamonds, emeralds and rubies – all glass but in their collectivity a treasure house, an Aladdin's cave. And in amidst these incredible structures the girls were enacting a play.

There were three characters: one a dark bearded villain, the other a young beggar of the streets, and lastly a princess. The young beggar tried to sing to the princess from his lowly station on the streets. She looked out from the balcony but ignored him. Then he did a host of marvellous things: flying here and there on carpets, destroying dragons and serpents, climbing mountains. All of this was clearly for the princess, who kept ignoring him. And then when the villain came to the princess on the balcony, with leering face and drawn scimitar, the young beggar flew to her rescue. She fell in love with him and he her. And then the villain lost his head and spent the rest of the play trying to find it.

Jean had advanced to the last table before the teacher's desk: He felt dazed, as though it was his own thoughts that were constructing the scenes before him. Here, across a bleak landscape of metal towers and walkways, tin machines warred like rival armies of ants. Roads and bridges pierced the air. Everywhere the whirring creatures rebounded from walls, clashed metal teeth, and whirred again in private clockwork reveries. There were no humans whatsoever and the landscape induced a sensation of despair. Here, the girls talked in lower voices. There was a sense that they were participating less in the construction of the creatures than the creatures were in producing themselves.

Jean left the buzz of conversation behind. He walked to the desk where the large woman sat. Close up, her hair rose upwards like the towers of paper theatres spiralling to the sky. As Jean stood apprehensively at the desk, her immense figure blocked out the blackboard behind her. Her voice echoed out over the little children like a foghorn.

After a few seconds Jean realised that she was made entirely of wax.

It was a shocking realisation. The mouth opened, but there was no person to speak, only an empty caricature with scary fixed eyes and a billowing empty dress that appeared to be blowing in some unfelt wind. Yet despite this, it remained realistic as though it had *been* a real woman.

'Who are you?' said the empty voice.

'I may ask the same question myself,' said Jean.

'Or answer it.'

'What are you?' said Jean suddenly.

'History,' said the thing in a clicky voice.

'And your class?'

'History.' The voice came out of the mouth. 'When I call their names they must respond or be part of the silence.'

'But this classroom is like Art.'

'Art,' said the voice, 'is where the actors make the audience.'

For some reason this reply gave Jean a very uneasy feeling. 'Do you mean literally make the people?' he asked.

'Yes, I do,' said the creature and the voice made a hollow hissing noise. 'Who are you?'

'Jean,'

'I asked who you are, not what you are called.'

'Who am I?' said Jean. 'If I knew, I would tell you.'

Moonster had followed behind him. 'He's Jean,' he said, 'a boy who chalks things and changes them. He's with me.'

'Ah, the messenger,' the voice came with a clicking and whirring. 'I know who *you* are.'

'The English master is dead,' Moonster said. 'There was an ...incident concerning time, or lack of it. He was killed along with his class.'

'Except Grimshaw the juggler,' said Jean hopefully.

Moonster's eyes filled with compassion. 'Except maybe the juggler.' But he looked uncertain. 'Guileless belief, the innocence of motion, sleight of hand. Perhaps amongst his many qualities he found one which could elude what other could not.'

'Jugglers have a way with time, something to do with illusion, space and movement,' said the head of History. 'I wish I could say the same for us. We are fixed here, making our little theatre plays from cardboard, metal and clay.'

'Do you have any message for me?' said Moonster.

The head thought for a while.

'Tell anyone who will listen that Time has a wallet in her back pocket, where she keeps change for oblivion. History spends the change in the hope of creating new worlds. Without change, there would be no new world.' She sighed. 'I can get the girls to make paper theatres...'

Moonster smiled. 'Would that we could all make new worlds so easily.'

One of the girls had rushed to the teacher. She was holding sheets of paper cut into beautiful identical shapes and formed into circular chains. The girl waited patiently, holding the shapes up.

'They're all the same,' said the teacher. 'In Art, they cut them from moulds and form them like these paper chains into exquisite shapes and forms but each identical. Only I paint them in their colours, all bright, all bright like a pageant.'

'Not all bright,' said Moonster.

'Allow one rhetoric,' replied the head of History. 'All those who encounter me are made bright. Let me paint you both.'

Moonster would not, but Jean allowed the girls to surround him. They took some of his uniform and painted it blue and yellow, so that the colours shone when he replaced it on his body. Jean felt altogether like a new man ready to face anything. The girls then surrounded him and placed a paper sword in his hands, a white shield on his arm and paper armour on his body; the whole being delicate, like marzipan icing on a wedding cake. Over his shoulders, they draped a fine cape made entirely from lace-like paper; a beautiful filigree, with stars and moons sewn or stuck over its whole length.

Then they brought a Banbury horse – a horse's head on a stick – but Jean refused to take it. Somehow, the horse appeared childish, but the rest did not. He felt comfortable dressed as a knight, even though he was only clad in paper.

'Perhaps it's a defence against Mara,' said Moonster. 'In any case, they seem to have chosen you as their champion.' He paused then added in a lower voice. 'I hope not as some kind of Fisher King.'

'But maybe,' said Jean, 'one of them knows where my sister has gone.'

'Ask.'

Jean tried to ask, but all the voices were raised and he could not make himself heard.

Moonster watched him with a critical eye, as the little girls formed a circle and began to dance in some ritualistic motion.

'I must pass this message on in some form or other,' said Moonster staring at the graceful weaving of their bodies as though the message might be contained in it.

The air became vivacious with song, a peculiar

190

chanting. The circling, singing girls came between Jean and Moonster like a stream bursting its banks.

'Meet me on the Bridge to Dreams,' Moonster shouted. The girls were thrusting them apart by sheer numbers. 'Next to the high water tower. You remember I pointed it out. Meet me there if you can.'

'But how will I find it?' shouted Jean.

'You will,' said Moonster.

Jean turned his attention back to the girls. 'Has anyone seen my sister... Michelle?' he asked. 'You call her *Papillon*.'

The girls continued their dance and began to push him with their bodies, towards the door.

The History teacher shouted out, before he reached the threshold. 'I saw her once. I see all things in time!'

But in the flurry and excitement, Jean found himself thrust out into the corridor, with the green carpet and the pools of light and the silence. For just one second, he watched the door close slowly like the pages of an illustrated fairy tale book. All the excited chatter died away, shut out like a story's ending.

'Just like Papa recorking a bottle of *Pineau*,' said Jean smiling to himself. He looked at the floor more closely. There, glinting in the light beside him, a tiny metal creature, made of tin with tiny legs was trying to get back into the room. Jean tried the door but it was firmly shut. Even as he pushed he heard the tumblers turn in the lock with an emphatic click.

Then again there was only silence and space and darkness, with little lights shining through the gloom to illuminate the way.

Feeling not very brave, a little silly, but also somewhat handsome in his paper armour, Jean began to stride up the corridor. There was a tiny clicking noise and the little tiny creature began to follow him. Jean smiled. 'Bridge to Dreams,' he said to the little creature, but it did not reply.

'Did Moonster point it out from his window? The only thing I know about it is that it's somewhere above me high up.'

The creature maintained its tiny silence.

Jean walked some way along the corridor without encountering anything of significance and then he saw a room door with 'ART' written above it. Here he could not resist a glimpse, so he slowly pushed open the door.

Instantly, he wished he had not. There was a smell that seemed composed of abattoirs, laboratories and hospitals all rolled into one. The room was over-bright and within it Jean saw dancing puppets, larger than human sized, made from paper with leering, malformed faces. They silently clacked their paper jaws together and sewed with ropes that appeared to be made of the strings that supported their bodies. These strings made a network, like the nest of a ship with pulleys, draws and chains. They soared upwards through a complicated series of lines into a ceiling shrouded in darkness. Jean felt like a little fly looking up at the canopy of an old spider web.

The ceiling was dark, but the flickering lights revealed human parts; legs, hands, faces and heads being sewn together slowly by the threads of the puppets.

Quickly and silently Jean closed the door.

'Art,' he thought with a shudder 'More like a slaughterhouse.'

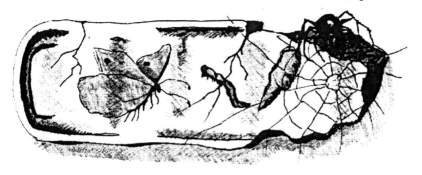

Chapter 20
The Reluctant Entomologist

Jean was still shuddering and looking backwards when he banged into something. Cases cascaded all around him and he was so dazed by this, he fell over.

'No, no my little one!' An angular figure stared down at him, dressed in a shabby black funereal jacket, chequered trousers and a conflicting bright blue waistcoat. The man seemed about to die of shock and Jean thought for a second that he had been mistaken for his long lost infant. Jean got up, and began to help pick up the cases, which were of different sizes, shapes and composition.

But the man shouted. 'Don't move. Don't move. As you live and breathe DON'T move!'

Jean froze, as with enormous circumspection and fragility, the angular man threw back his cape and produced some forceps and a magnifying glass from under his mortarboard. He reached down to the floor. There was a moment of intense inspection, an unbelievably quick flurry of movement, and then the man picked up a tiny thing and placed it in a neat matchbox.

'Thank goodness,' said the man. 'That was so close.

Now, you must help those you encounter and especially those whom you have previously hindered.' Without looking back he continued, he began to walk away, saying, 'the cases – to my room.'

It was a short journey, which was fortunate, as Jean felt as if he were carrying the contents of an entire vivarium in his arms. He could hear buzzing and scratching emerging from the cases, as though a thousand incarcerated novelists had just found inspiration. In one or two of the glass ones (one of which was lodged against his nose) some large spiders vied for courage with Jean. But neither the spiders not Jean could escape each other's company for the moment.

Down a set of short steps, they came to a lavish door. Here the angular man turned about. 'What's your name, boy?'

'Jean.'

'Mine's Crimp – new master of Entomology. Both new boys, eh?'

Jean nodded from behind the cases.

'You nearly lost my Patsy! But let's not hold that against forming an alliance in this grim establishment.' He held out his hand.

Jean stared at it over a spider, grown more puzzled than timid. 'Jean,' he repeated with a hopeless look.

'Ah, I see. Let's wait for formalities.' Crimp produced a key. 'As you live and breathe,' he said with emphasis, 'don't touch anything, move anywhere, or look in anything without prior advice.'

Beyond a door shaped from rare sandalwood they entered a dim lit room.

'Cases there,' said Crimp, indicating a bench that ran along the length of one wall. In seconds, Crimp categorised and labelled the boxes into various groups. Speaking in a high voice to no one in particular with hands that seemingly performed actions independent of his mind, he put every box into its final resting place.

While he watched Crimp work, Jean took in the room. It was constructed like the inside of a turret or chimney and rose into shadowed eaves lost in darkness. But immediately before and around him, lit with hidden spotlights, were large workbenches, which were covered in killing-jars, bottles of various solutions, labels and nets. On each bench, rows of pins, like the swords of miniature advancing phalanxes, rose up from spreading-boards. Above the benches, and surrounding all the walls like caskets in a Spanish cemetery, were a series of carefully labelled Schmitt boxes. Here Crimp stashed, threw or spurned a resting spot for each case with the elegance and accuracy of an acrobatic juggler. He was like a frenetic Grimshaw.

There were steps and ladders leading upwards into the gloom, as though at one time the whole room had been some kind of primitive lighthouse. On every wall-space the boxes, cases and drawers rose into infinity. As Jean peered upwards into the gloom, he realised that Crimp had began talking in an excited voice.

'You'll only see Patsy in school during autumn and a part of winter, until the cold becomes severe. But she comes early to the fields. On the first fine day in February, you shall see her warming herself even against the sun-blessed walls of this old school. I saw her in considerable numbers on the laurustinus. That's where she made her first assignations.' He whipped a bright smile towards Jean. 'While sipping the sugar of the small white flowers, much as we sip claret with a young lady.' He laughed. 'Too early for the young ladies for you, Jean?'

Jean realised that Crimp did not really expect an answer from him. He had picked up a Berlese funnel in one hand and a colander in the other, and appeared to be literally weighing their value.

'The whole of the summer season is spent out of doors, in brief flights from one flower to the next, like a debutante on her first spring season,' Crimp whispered. 'Then, when autumn comes, she retires like some exhausted belle to the country. She makes her way into our classrooms and remains until the hard frosts. And then my boys *will* bring me their little presents. Their little paper bags. Their little captures. Which is why we are so lucky to have Patsy here now.' He held forth a jar containing a tiny slothful bluebottle and then cradled it with motherly caress. 'Thus do I fill my vivarium.' He pointed to some large, bell-shaped cages of wire-gauze that stood in earthenware pans. Next to one of them was a small glass case, containing a dish that held a dead bird. When Jean moved closer he could see that the cages were full of moving sand.

'But still they must have their delicacies,' said Crimp. He pointed to a cup of golden honey on one of the desks. 'Here my little captives will come to occupy themselves in their hours of leisure. To nurture them I will employ small birds – linnets, chaffinches, sparrows, which, regrettably, I must have shot. Fortunately, I came prepared.' He pointed distastefully to the small dish. Then he threw off his cape, took a walking cane that he had placed against the bench, threw it spiritedly into a stand with upside-down sweep nets and umbrellas, and began a little comic dance.

'Look here,' Crimp continued. 'I have just served up a linnet shot two days ago. I next place in the case, Patsy, *notre dame.*' He held up the little jar. 'Look at her fat belly. Soon she will be a mother. In an hour, when the excitement of being put in prison is allayed, Patsy will be in labour. With eager, jerky steps, she will explore her new home from head to tail, then returning from the tail to the head, she will repeat the action several times, and at last settle near an eye.' Crimp paused, then said, 'This is not upsetting you, is it?' It was as if he had become aware of sensibilities that might differ from his own.

Jean shook his head. He felt that he had largely gone beyond the possibility of being upset.

'Good.' Crimp looked a little uneasy, as though he was about to say something indelicate. He licked his lips. 'Her ovipositor will bend at a right angle and drive in straight down to the root. Then her eggs will be emitted for nearly half an hour. During this we... I am nothing to her.' Crimp had begun to weep. 'Several times over, she will return to the same spot...' He searched for a handkerchief. 'But don't you see, Jean, the awful truth?'

Jean shook his head.

'She *dies* the next day.' Crimp broke down, his head buried in his arms, his body shaking with convulsions. 'She dies.'

'It's only a fly,' thought Jean.

'I know what you are thinking,' said Crimp, when he finally raised his head. 'You're thinking it's *only* a fly. But it's not only a fly. It was the chaffinch too and then it will be the maggots and as you live and breathe, you won't...' He broke down again.

Jean found another handkerchief on the bench and passed it to the wilting form. Crimp picked out a unit tray from a Cornell drawer. There were three spiders in it. 'Look.' he said. 'It's not only the fly. It's the whole room. Each of these drawers is full to the brim. In each of these boxes, there are innumerable tiny insects and each one will die. They *are* dying, even as we watch.'

Jean felt a gulp in his throat. He saw again the tiny cocoon on the back porch at Auntie May's and its twin in the stockroom cobweb: dying butterflies, dying fathers, everything and everyone hurtling towards an abyss

'Don't you see?' said Crimp. 'As you love the chaffinch so much, you love the worm. If you love the sweetest girl, you must also love the fly, which will...'

Suddenly a shadow threw itself across the whole room and for a second Jean thought that the world was about to be blotted out.

'Crimp, need any assistance?' A gaunt master of middle age, holding his mortarboard, clad in a worn brown suit with a tattered cape, was staring sternly into the room.

Crimp was unable to speak. He sat holding his knees.

The master entered the room. 'It's Shave,' he said.

In the space that followed Jean had incredible images of the master wielding a razor in some ghastly ritual, but then the voice spoke again more insistently. 'Shave from Physics. Here to help you shift these spiders and escort you to the debate. You *are* going, Crimp? You know attendance is expected, particularly from new masters?'

Crimp still did not speak. He sighed loudly, reached for the handkerchief and blew in to it.

Shave looked around the walls with a masterful eye. 'No one ever likes the entomologist's post I suppose. It's all these damned spiders.' He looked warily up at the walls. 'Boxes full of bloody spiders.' He stared at Jean as if he were going to be contradicted. 'Imagine, boy, if we all had to go about worrying about bloody spiders in a box. Where would be then?'

'We wouldn't have to worry,' said Crimp, rallying. 'Because unless we opened the boxes we would never know we had a spider.'

'Rubbish,' said Shave.

'No,' said Crimp. 'Suppose everyone had a box with a spider in it, and you weren't able to look in anyone else's box. We might all have different things in our boxes that

198

we were calling "spider" but...'

'I had a little beetle, Alexander was its name,' said Jean suddenly.

The two masters looked at him as if he were insane.

Crimp seemed to have entirely recovered his poise. He gave Jean a censorious look. 'The thing in the box has no place in the game at all, not even as a something: for the box might even be empty. "Spider" might mean "empty" in one person's language and "worm" in another person's language. One would never know until the box was opened. And therefore if one carried a box around with something one called a spider in it, we need not worry about it one little bit!'

'But you should worry,' said Jean.

'Why?' said Crimp and Shave together.

'Because *you* had to carry the box,' replied Jean.

'Hmm,' murmured Crimp.

Shave nodded his head wisely. 'Unless the box was merely an idea. And then, think, if we dropped all the boxes and the various things escaped, where would be?' He gave Jean a significant glance and then looked again at the walls, shuddering. He laid one hand on a Cornell drawer. 'These specimens are fading even in this light,' he said. 'The Head won't be impressed.'

'These ones are dead,' replied Crimp, and his chin began to lower again.

'The Head wants all of the dead specimens transferred up there,' Shave intoned. He gave a nod to indicate upwards.

'As I live and breathe, I can't be responsible for the dead.'

'He won't expect you to be responsible, only to deliver them,' said Shave. 'Best go to the debate. Leave the cases until after lunch. We are already late.'

Crimp leapt to his feet, picked up his field notes and adjusted the case where Patsy was already settling in. He turned to Jean. 'You'd best be off to class, young man,' he said. 'As I live and breathe, don't touch anything, move anywhere or look in anything without prior advice.'

Shave pushed a false wall in a column of case shelvings and disappeared with Crimp down a dark tunnel beyond. The false wall slid back and Jean was left with the insects.

For a while Jean sat resting, but the room was not conducive to rest. All the while he could hear the rustling and twittering of incarcerated insects, like the tiny scraping files of hopeful escapologists. He jumped up and shook himself. The room felt oppressive, as if at any moment there would be a sudden mass escape and the whole interior would be thronged with bees, wasps and other things that stung or bit.

Jean glanced at the nearest bench. It was labelled 'Aquatic Creatures' and a brief survey of the whirligigs, water striders, backswimmers and other less prepossessing but bigger insects was enough to make him forget about lunch.

Strewn all over the surface of the benches were various insect traps. 'This whole place is one big trap,' thought Jean. He found a microscope. There were a series of them along the left hand wall, mostly covered by leather hoods, but this one was uncovered and by coincidence, it was labelled 'Lower Debating Room.' This seemed so unusual that Jean, despite Crimp's warnings, he just had to look.

Chapter 21
The Great Debate

I have often regretted my speech, never my silence.

- Xenocrates

At first Jean thought he was staring at a virus slide. There were wriggling chaotic shapes squirming before his eye. Then these resolved and all he could see were spiders, beetles, butterflies, dragonflies – a whole plethora of insect life. But when Jean shook his head all that was gone. In its place he saw a large hall teeming with red-blazered pupils and black-gowned masters. This gave Jean the impression that some giant had nearly completed an enormous jigsaw of a ladybird.

There seemed to be a great commotion, as if someone was about to be hanged and half the assembly was in violent opposition. Then Jean gasped. The scene was resolving by some peculiar magic. He could see faces now, faces that he recognised. There was Moonster carrying his coloured file, seated on a low bench at the side below the stage. There was Grimshaw at the front still holding his hoops. Incredibly, he stood beside the

201

Master of English and some of the pupils who Jean knew were already dead. There were others, masters and pupils and they all looked tense and drawn. There came a sudden rap as of a hammer hitting wood and a voice cried out, 'Silence please for the debate. Chair is Mr Shave. Proponents of the motion are master of English, Mr Lawrence, and student Marcus Poloni.'

There was a thin cheer and Jean saw the English master walk to the platform. He was followed by the thin boy whom Jean recalled standing on the balcony above the garden.

'Those opposing the motion,' continued the voice, 'are Master Chef, Bulboon, and his sculley, Broadbent.'

A sullen silence, suggestive more of poor rations than philosophy fell on the hall as a towering fat man dressed entirely in white and sporting an apron that looked like a hanging curtain was followed on to the stage by a young boy of such contrasting proportions that he was for a moment entirely hidden by the former's body. The two struggled into postion like short sighted actors looking for stage markers. Comic possibilities presented themselves at every contorted movement but ultimately failed to materialise.

The hall settled. The invisible owner of the voice cried, 'This house supports the motion:"Buns: Food for thought?"'

Lawrence, the English master, had risen to his feet during the announcement, but he stopped dead as he was about to reach the lectern. It was abundantly apparent that this was not the motion for which he had prepared. He took the last few steps hesitantly and then gripped the lectern with his big hands. There was an instant where he seemed to have lost his resolve. Then he began to speak in his melodious deep-timbred voice. 'I was under the impression that we were debating the institution of the new library, a much needed school resource but... if that is how things stand, let us discuss the motion before us,' he paused, '...however, absurd.'

The air was stilled, the audience overcome both with the majesty of his presence and the insinuation that he was about to say something contrary.

'Thinking is an art, speech its vehicle' said Lawrence. 'Buns are food, the vehicle for the body's nutrition. The body requires buns, the buns impel thought, thought impels speech and speech transforms the world and leads, in the hands of the wise, to the enlightenment of the less gifted. In short, through speech we come to the truth. Truth is only truly found, however, when the proof is in the pudding: through medicine, when it effects a cure, through gymnastics when it effects a victory, through justice when it is done, and through legislation, which brings about a just state of conditions and allows the possibility of justice.' He paused again and his shifting eyes took in the whole assembly. 'A condition which many would like to observe in the immediate establishment.'

It was a risk. He had taken it. His small frame swelled with precarious power. Mr Lawrence of English sat down to tremendous applause.

'Bulboon against,' said Shave in a small voice, when the applause had receded.

Bulboon blinked, seemingly unaware of his surroundings. Broadbent nudged him. He rose to his preposterously small feet, advanced like a drunken man to the lectern, held it in his hands, and surveyed the waiting audience with a surly glance. '*Merde*,' he said in loud voice. He returned to his chair and sat down in belligerent triumph.

There was a hesitant response, a subdued disapproval.

'Marcus Poloni to second the motion "Buns: food for

thought",' said Shave.

Imbued with the arrogance of youth, Poloni gave Bulboon a disdainful stare, walked foppishly to the lectern, took off his white gloves and placed them in his top blazer pocket. 'I had expected to formulate an argument in offence to opponents of "Bun's food for thought?" Instead, I must set forth a further attack on the legitimacy of any opposing view. What is at stake here is the very nature of truth.' Poloni smashed one hand onto the lectern and winced. Recovering his poise, he stared directly at Broadbent as though anticipating that the final assault might come from just such an insidious source. He pointed his finger wildly. 'There are many forms of flattery, which might be employed, many cosmetics that would paint a weak argument, appeals to the senses rather than mind, appeals to taste rather than nutrition. But for the body to work, it needs buns. Need I add that it also needs more staple foods: proteins, soups, pottages, broils, grills...'

The audience was applauding with vigour.

When the applause receded, Poloni wiped his sweating forehead. 'Let no sophistry from our opponents subdue the clarity of your response. Let no bald, unfounded rhetoric confuse you. Vote for Buns. Food for thought!"

Broadbent had difficulty making himself heard. The applause continued all the way to the lectern. It continued until he raised his hand, as Shave begged for silence. In a voice as thin and wheezing as his body, he blurted his response. 'To be a speaker, one must rely upon rhetoric. Rhetoric cannot lead one toward knowledge of the truth. Therefore, when one speaks, it is impossible to make decisions based upon the speech that lead toward truth. There is only one solution to this dilemma and Master Chef Bulboon provides it – buns, buns for the eating, buns for the savouring and not just buns, CREAM BUNS, today and all week, will be served in the hall! Is there a need to vote?'

The deluge of applause for this final statement precluded further debate. Jean watched in dumbfoundment. He saw Poloni jumping to his feet shouting, 'Transform, transmute!' in a despairing echo of his master's voice. He heard a bell ringing. He watched in stupefaction as the scene resolved itself like a kaleidoscope; one instant a hall bustling with human faces, the next a swirling host of insects and finally, as his eyes began to retreat from the microscope, he saw a slide teeming with viruses in a swirling body.

Jean staggered back, hearing a second bell. This time, it was in the world immediately around him. Even as he fell back, almost as though shoved, he heard the scraping of chairs mingled with the clacking of the tiny incisors of insects. He scrabbled to his feet and fought for the exit, aware only that at any moment the whole turret room might explode into a vast conglomeration of insects, all with the single goal of eating him alive.

As Jean burst out into the corridor, he became immediately aware that the bell had ceased to ring, that the corridor was profoundly empty and that all that remained of any crowd was the tiny metal creature. It had waited like a patient dog for its master and seemed as pleased to see Jean as any living being. Jean patted it quickly on the head. Without pause, he began to pace along the corridor. The little creature trailed happily behind.

Now a new intensity came to the air. At intervals the creeping cold began to numb Jean's feet and he knew that somewhere Mara infested a dimension close at hand in its efforts to find him. Jean had an intuition that the thing was not conscious in the sense that a human or even an animal was conscious. Perhaps it homed in on vitality. Perhaps it simply needed to eat the present. Jean rushed past classrooms always looking for a way to higher areas.

And then she came to Jean, at first silent, then low like a tiny, beating heart intruding itself on his mind. Then like the galloping of horses far away, but growing louder like the beating of a drum: the temporal machine, Mara, stealer of memories was battering the air and space around Jean from its unseen source.

Jean turned around. A thin mist had begun to rise from the floor. The carpet was giving way, melting, churning up like the beginnings of turbulence in a previously calm sea. Goose pimples rose on Jean's flesh, as he watched the tiny tin creature, caught in the billowing impossible mist, crumble to rust.

Before Jean's eyes the temporal machine, in all its amorphism, began to manifest.

Jean drew his paper sword and stood ready to face it.

Then he screamed and ran.

The thought had occurred to him that a paper sword was not the best defence against a thing that appeared to eat flesh as he might eat a raspberry.

Jean ran, and rooms flashed past him as though he were a fairground horse spiralling around the funfair. There was only one way ahead, and as Jean came to the end of the corridor, he saw the foot of a stairway. Here, the mist rose belligerently. Jean glanced quickly over his shoulder and realised that the thing was on his heels at every step. He could hear the voices in the mist; pleading, begging, accusing.

And then the stair – dark and forbidding – was before him. He gasped with relief. 'Up,' Jean thought. 'Maybe it can't go up stairs.'

Jean jumped upwards, two steps at a time. When he reached the first landing, he turned and saw that the mists and the voices had also risen. They followed him slowly; anonymous, bilious and sickening. Jean stared wildly around himself. The landing was hemmed in by a single Cornell drawer, dead butterflies pinned to its spreading boards faded in the light of a long church-like window. Jean paused, fought for breath. He felt an instinctive dread of the contents of the Cornell drawers, a dread that nearly outweighed his fear of the approaching mist. 'Up,' he thought. 'It's the only way.' And then he saw the sign.

He stopped in stupefied shock.

It was simply an arrow

THE HEAD

But it apparently pointed to the Head's room. He now saw that there was a low door on the right of the Cornel drawers.

Below Jean, the mists of the temporal machine crept up the stairs like the multiple tentacles of a phantom squid. Sweat broke out on Jean's forehead. And then he saw another sign, obscured by dust and age, below that of the arrow. He rubbed it.

EXIT

To the left of the Cornel drawers there was a dark passageway. Beyond that he could now see what might be a door in the distance. 'Left,' he thought. 'It has to be left.' Stooping, he entered the left hand corridor. He broke into a run. Anything was better than the Head's room. Behind him the mist seemed vitalised by the nearness of the room, as a devotee takes power from a hallowed relic. An oppressive gloom pervaded the whole area. The corridor narrowed. There was an exit. Some kind of fire door. Old brass bars were locked together, stiff. Jean turned. There was no retreat. The mist billowed forward, sighing, weeping, begging, burgeoning out in the enclosed space. Controlling his panic as best he could, Jean turned his back on the mist. He pushed, very hard. It was no good. And then, as the first tendrils of the whispering mist curled around his feet, he jumped at the bars. They caved in and he was through, into the glaring light of day. He had found an exit from the confines of the school.

Here in that instant he was propelled onto an old stairwell, a fire escape of iron steps. He could go up or down but he must act quickly. Turning Jean slammed the door behind him. He thrust forward, but one of his feet plunged through the rusted metal steps. The step slashed his leg. The bright blood made him stop, but more so the fact that he was trapped. He looked down. Was the mist rising through the gap beneath the fire door, or was it his imagination? He tried to free his leg but it was really stuck. Shards of tetanus-bearing rust stuck out like a frozen explosion around his calf.

Above, he heard footsteps, a heavy slow tread with measured careful steps.

The angle in which his leg had been trapped made it possible to see below and to his left. Below, the mist appeared to be dissipating but he could not be sure. To his left Jean could see the rising walls of the inner court, a ledge and then a drop to the roof of the greenhouse some distance below. There was no escape. His fingers scrabbled around the metal gap.

He could do nothing.

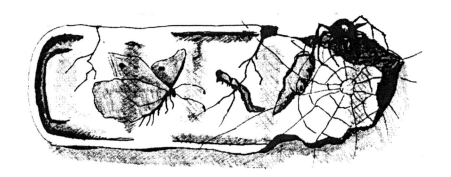

Chapter 22
The Master of Geography

Under the wide and starry sky. Dig
the grave and let me lie.
- Adlai E. Stevenson

Jean heard a flat ringing noise, like the sound of a slow bell. It was coming from above, ponderously, as if it found the whole world heavy.

Two leather-bound feet, big feet, stopped at the step below Jean's face. The shoes had large pillars of trousers attached. The belly was too fat for Jean to see anything more, except a long flowing black cape.

'The Head,' Jean gasped. He did not mean to say it, but it came out.

'Only of Geography, young man.' The voice was low and deep like the rumble of a distant and ancient train. 'How interesting.'

'Sore,' said Jean. If he was going to die he thought he may as well die sarcastically.

'Sore, I expect, but still interesting.'

Jean said nothing.

'A paper knight. One doesn't see many paper knights

209

nowadays.'

'I expect not.'

'On the fire escape? What are you doing here, young man?'

'Escaping Mara, the temporal machine. '

'Temporal machine? How interesting. And you intended to escape by placing your leg in that gap. I would think that you might have had a better chance by avoiding it.'

'It was a mistake. I pushed my foot through by mistake.'

'Why didn't you say? *Interesting*. Would you like me to free you?'

'Can you?'

'That remains to be seen.' The large plump hands reached down and inserted a metal ruler between the rust and Jean's foot. One hand gripped Jean's leg and the other manipulated the ruler like an old shoehorn, removing Jean's leg from the jagged hole.

Jean was in considerable pain, not to mention feeling worried, but he was lucid enough to inspect his rescuer. He looked up to see the biggest man he had ever seen. The body was not gross, not fat; just huge. The legs themselves seemed to stretch to the moon and the boots were bigger than those of Frankenstein's monster. There was a sense of enormous strength; not the strength of a muscle man or a gymnast, but the kind of old strength in an ancient tree trunk. Jean just knew that the wind could blow as much as it wanted, but all it would ever do is ripple the clothes around this huge man. It would be like a zephyr trying to tease the bark from a tree. From his boots to his cape the master was dressed in black, but his face was pure white; bloodless with thin hair swept back over a white brow and two slit eyes framing a thin nose. His full, scarlet lips broke open into a huge nervous grin, revealing ivory white teeth that were like the keys of a piano. His face was like but unlike that of the Head's portrait Jean had seen so long ago.

'Thanks,' said Jean. 'Will I get tetanus?'

'Oh yes,' said the master. 'But there's a cure for everything.'

He held out his enormous hands. 'You had better come up to my classroom.' He took Jean by the hand and led him up the fire escape.

'I don't trust him,' thought Jean 'but what do I do?'

Each step seemed as though it might break the iron stairs. The rust crumbled and fell away in brown flakes to the ground. Jean looked up uneasily and saw in the far distance the rope basket slung from Moonster's high room. But Moonster was not there. He knew by looking at the rope, and where it ended – a little below him and to the south – that the 'Bridge to Dreams' must be close, perhaps a little to the north and up.

Jean wanted to go there immediately, but the mere presence of the huge Geography master was like a magnet he could not escape. He followed the retreating back like a tug following a cargo ship until they came to a balcony similar to the one where he'd met the English class, but this was bare of any decorations or furniture. The master opened the door to the room beyond, and Jean walked behind him. The big man had to stoop low as he crossed the threshold.

'Must bang his head a lot,' thought Jean.

The classroom inside was dominated by a huge globe that stood in the centre of the room. When Jean examined it, he could see no familiar landmasses or seas. Instead, it appeared to map out classrooms, gutters, roofs and playing fields. He tried to look further for the garden, but it was either not there or on the far side of the globe. Quickly, he glanced at the rest of his surroundings.

There was nothing else remarkable. The room was empty of pupils. It had an air of tired calm, like a snoozing elderly relative catching a moment's rest. Jean had not been invited to sit but he went to a desk at the front of the classroom and risked sitting on it. For a while he stared at his injured leg and then he looked at the desk. It was unremarkable except that it was old and not covered in graffiti.

The huge man pottered around at his desk for a while. Then he came over to Jean and absently handed him a plaster. After this, he returned to his desk. Jean thought the Geography master was going to write on the empty blackboard, but instead he began to adjust and fiddle with a complicated series of pulleys beside it. There was a moment when the room seemed to become unnaturally still and then there was a great whirring and crunching of gears and cogs and wheels. Slowly, the blackboard parted down the middle like the opening doors of a lift. The late afternoon sun shone through the gap, beyond which Jean saw two immense towers.

Sunlight fell on a vast hidden courtyard, which was flagged in old stone. At various points along its plane, intersected by a gravel path, buildings sprouted like monuments. In all, it appeared as though a giant ocean had drawn back and left an abundance of carbuncles, winkles and limpets in even spaces along the deserted stone.

There was a silence, a deadly silence, about the whole scene. Jean's mouth went dry, and the hairs on his neck rose. He had been dealing with unreality for some time. This landscape seemed somehow *too* real.

The Geography master turned and smiled his huge smile, then walked through the gap in the blackboard. He stood motionless for a moment, like a figure in a huge surreal, religious painting. In that moment, Jean realised what the eruptions in the flagged courtyard were and a shudder ran through his whole body.

'Geography!' said the master, but Jean knew that it was a different form of geography from anything that he had previously encountered. The huge figure beckoned to him and he had to follow. They walked a short way into the courtyard and into a new and ghastly form of silence. The flags beneath Jean's his feet were unnaturally hot, but the air was crisp, not stifling. They stepped onto the gravel path.

The master turned towards him. 'Geography is the art of space management,' he said through his red lips.

'I thought it was the study of land.'

'It's not the land we study. It's the spaces in between.'

'But this is a graveyard,' said Jean.

'No bigger spaces than in a graveyard.'

'Who's buried here?' Jean really did not want to know the answer to this, but he felt he had to find out.

'Everyone is buried in here,' replied the master. 'Masters and pupils.'

'Is this a secret place?'

'Not any more. Although I hear it said that there are secrets here.'

'Can I look at the graves?'

'That is why I opened it up.'

Jean began to pick his way among the mausoleums; some small, some large. The sun shone ominously above and made pools of darkness open up; in the long shadows of the mausoleums, a stillness spilled like ink. As Jean walked, he noticed that the graves were all jumbled up. They appeared to have recent dates and old dates, and the ages of the deceased varied from ten to one hundred and twenty. The graves were all beneath the flagstones and the mausoleums were raised above them, sometimes surrounded by iron grills with great padlocks.

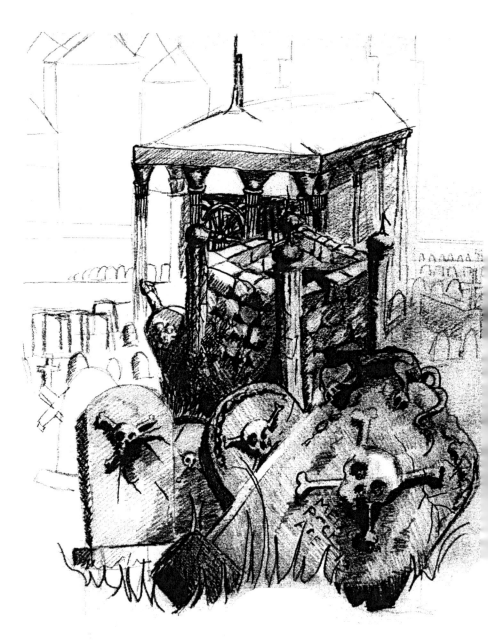

"Who's burid here?"

'Who would rob the graves?' Jean thought. Then he remembered Biology and his stomach churned.

On top of the graves, lizards basked easily in the sun, their green armoured bodies reflecting the light like emeralds. They did not move when he approached and Jean became aware suddenly of a thousand eyes staring at him. A shadow lumbered beside him.

'What are you looking for?' said the master.

'My sister, Michelle. They call her *Papillon* here.'

The big figure nodded. Jean kept walking, looking at the names.

He came finally to the centre of the yard, where a broad gravelled path struck out in either direction. Here there was a small Renaissance fountain, and around its base an old withered rose bush had wrapped itself like the beginnings of Sleeping Beauty's forest. The fountain was empty, dry.

'If a gravestone topples here and there is no ear to hear it does it make a sound?' said the master abstractly.

'There are always ears here,' replied Jean in irritation.

'You are a lot sharper than you look, young man.'

The rose bush trailed across the path, resting at the bottom of some marble steps that led to the doors of a great mausoleum, almost like a Greek or Egyptian tomb, which rested in the corner of the cross made by the path's intersection. Four Doric columns supported a huge plinth, and an architrave stretched around the tomb, depicting a pattern of what looked like insects, maggots and flies. In the centre of the plinth, a column was placed which supported at its summit a large statue, diminished by height and perspective, holding a book and pointing to the heavens. The statue had such a precarious hold on gravity that Jean found it difficult to look at. But he was drawn to this tomb, which acted more like a magnet than the huge Geography master. Jean followed the trail of the rose bush until he reached the bottom step. When he saw that the architrave was depicting the life cycle of a butterfly he knew that his search for his sister was nearly over.

'*Papillon,*' he said and he found it interesting that he could no longer call her Michelle. These words were engraved on the foot of the architrave.

Papillon
The Seventh Silence

The statue, although worn and crumbling with the elements, depicted an idealised form of his sister as the young woman she might have become.

The master stood beside him. 'They built it for her.'

'Who?'

'The pupils of the school. They all provided pocket money, a penny each.'

'But it's old, very old.'

'It was a long time ago.'

Jean looked at the white drawn face of the master. The windless space appeared to make him more fragile, as though he might burst like a balloon if pricked.

'But I saw her when I first came here. I know it was her.'

'Know. Know,' said the master. 'Tell me, what does the caterpillar know of the butterfly?'

'As much as the butterfly knows of the cocoon,' said Jean gritting his teeth, not wanting to be deflected. 'I tell you I saw her.'

'But that was a long time ago too.'

'The temporal machine, Mara. Did it touch me too?' said Jean to himself.

'In the end it touches us all,' said the master. 'It's how you live that counts, not how quickly.'

Jean walked a little closer to the step, placed one foot on it and examined the iron grille that stretched across the front of the portico. 'Why did they want all this built?'

'To remember her.'

'But why?'

'Because... they needed her.'

On the edge of his consciousness Jean felt a sigh that seemed to emerge from the rows upon rows of graves. He felt tears welling. A terrible pain began in his stomach, which he wanted to get out but could not. It made his heart ache and his eyes burn. His heart was a well and he was slipping into it. His eyes were hurting with the light and yet he could see an old pool of darkness in his mind that wanted to expand until it consumed him, or worse, became him. 'I must see,' he said.

'Of course,' said the master. He waited respectfully as Jean gathered himself.

'What does it mean?' said Jean eventually. 'The Seventh Silence?'

'Some say there are many forms of silence. One is the silence of a graveyard and the other is the silence of a grave.' The master pulled a long chain of keys from his pocket and without hesitation unlocked the rusted padlock on the iron grille. With hardly any effort he pushed the grille apart, with a terrible creaking and grinding, which echoed in the depths of the tomb. Jean could not help noticing that between the bars of the grille there were thick old spider webs containing countless corpses of flies and coloured butterflies. They festooned the tomb like an inappropriate garland. He brushed the tears from his eyes and drew the paper sword from its paper scabbard. 'I'm going in.'

217

'I'm not,' said the master. 'It's too scary.'

Jean knew that if he waited any longer he would not do it, so he took a gulp and walked into the black depths.

There was a bare passage only about two meters long, undecorated. Beyond it, Jean could see an even blacker hole where he guessed there must be steps. 'Are there steps?' Jean asked over his shoulder.

'How would I know?' said the master's voice. It had changed, as though the air of the tomb had made the outside world less real.

Jean walked forward a little, his eyes getting used to the darkness.

Then there was another creaking and grinding. He turned quickly only to see the gates slamming shut, the key turning in the padlock.

'Works every time,' said the master.

Jean ran back, gripped the bars and pulled. They shook and the chain appeared to be laughing at him. The master was not. He stared with pitiless eyes in a drawn white face. His black clothes were like a pallbearer's costume, and his face looked more and more like a white skull. And now, although Jean had not realised it before, he saw that the master's trousers were not truly black. They were chequered. 'You!' said Jean.

'Who?'

'The Head. You've aged and somehow *grown*. But you *are* the Head.'

'Only of Geography.'

'But you said yourself that Geography was the study of the spaces in between. And the space in between is death.'

'Think what you wish. That's your choice.'

Jean spat between the bars. He missed the face of the master, whose expression remained unchanged.

'And my choice now?'

The master smiled. 'What choice does anyone have in

a tomb? The dead are only accomplished waiters.'

Jean gripped the bars until his hands whitened. He stared in frustration at the even smile on the impassive face. He thought of his father, his mother, his sister. His head roared with pumping blood. The dark corner of his mind expanded like a bleeding wound. Jean fought it. I'm not waiting,' he said. 'Watch me.'

With one look of hatred and defiance, Jean turned and walked back down the passageway.

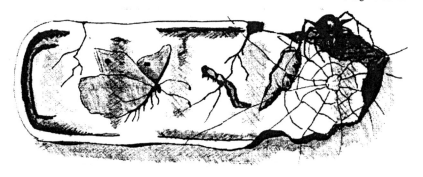

Chapter 23
A Leap in the Dark

When you gaze long into the abyss,
the abyss also gazes into you.
- Friedrich Nietzsche

Jean didn't cry. He waited for a while in the darkness,
until gradually steps revealed themselves to his
adjusting eyes, as if someone had begun to uncover a
series of muted lights. So, there *were* steps and they led
down. Jean placed one foot forward and then the next.
One, two, three, four steps. The dimness here was
virtually impenetrable. His courage departed to be
replaced by a growing fear. Jean breathed in a deep
musty smell and heard the sound of dripping moisture,
far away. Each step seemed worse than the last. He was
walking into nothing, and at any time he expected to
disappear into an abyss or to find a stray Goobley or
other monster about to eat him.

Jean descended twenty steps and then banged into a
wall. At first, he thought it was a dead end. He allowed
his fingers to travel over its damp surface. Things
scurried in the darkness. His fingers touched something
soft that plopped to the ground. His mouth was dry. He

waited a little and then explored. It was a corner. The steps turned at right angles, still going down, down. After a while, he came to another wall. Again the steps turned. Jean paused. Below he could see green light. *See?* How could he see? The steps became clearer and then he was there.

Struck by a shaft of green light, a tomb lay in the centre of a small chamber. All along the walls, just above head height, ran a series of engravings whose subject mirrored that depicted on the external architrave of the mausoleum: a butterfly, a caterpillar, a pupa, endlessly repeated. The sound of dripping came from an outlet of water falling from a long stone flute that hung from the darkness of the ceiling. The water dripped into a chalice at the head of a stone figure, carved in the likeness of a slim crusader, which was embedded in the rock of the tomb. The source of the smell appeared to be the small fungi and mosses festooning the dank walls.

Slowly, Jean advanced, feeling as he had years before when he and his father had entered the *Basilque Sainte Madeleine* and had stood before the reliquary in the hallowed silence of the crypt. Jean felt he could almost touch the sacred air surrounding the tomb. And he sensed that others had knelt here in awe and dread, in the silence and peace of sacred worship, believing, hoping, wishing and searching. He dreaded to break the silence even if only by placing his feet on the stone floor.

The green light came from above. For a second, it dimmed, and Jean realised that it must come from the sky. Perhaps there was an opening in the roof of the tomb far above, which allowed the trapped sunlight to filter into the chamber and to fall directly on the face of the sleeping crusader.

Jean stared. Was it his sister? He could not tell. It was a knight dressed in armour, legs crossed mid shin, sword over her breast. He had seen the like in small

222

chapels around southern France. He said 'her' to himself. It was a girl or a young boy, not a man, but the face was concealed in a mask. A visor covered the features, leaving only a slit for the eyes.

Jean knelt on the cold floor. He looked up at the shaft of light. It wavered at times as though a hand was caressing the light, trapping it and then freeing it to spill into the chamber. When the green light shone, Jean felt as though the chamber was full of sweet air and the smell of spices, fragrant and tantalising, filled his whole being. When it faded, a rank smell spilled out and the fungi protruding from the mosses became like small gnomish heads bickering in the gloom. Jean felt then that the light would never return and he would die alone and miserable in a tomb beneath the stone courtyard.

For a long time Jean kneeled, meditating, trying to still his thoughts, but they were too insistent.

The master, the head of Geography, whatever he thought he was, had believed that this was the end of all things. Did he know of the tomb? He said he was scared of it. He thought the place was silent, but he could never know that the tomb was alive with a cacophony of thoughts. Jean knew that this was not where the search for silence ended, whatever that search might be. Did the master know of the light? Somehow Jean thought he could not know. Slowly, he raised himself to his feet. Was there more to the chamber than he thought? Was it like the Queen's Chamber in the Great Pyramid of Cheops, concealing secrets beyond the limited imagination of others? Was there a key for a lock that he had missed?

Jean walked around the room examining the architecture. The carvings were old. He felt them with his chilling fingers. Was there a secret spring that concealed a hidden chamber? There were some unusual holes in the architrave. He tried everything, even inserting the old key for the stockroom cupboard back in Park Grammar into some of the likely holes. Hopelessly, he tried his back door key. Nothing worked. He walked again to the walls. He knocked on each one, searching for hollow places. All he found was a single loose flagging. When he prised it up, there was only dank earth beneath it. He tried to dig with his fingers but the ground was too hard.

Jean walked back to the centre of the chamber. The sides of the tomb were bare except for some Latin inscription.

Aqua Est Vita

Here was the chalice. He touched it. It appeared unmoveable. He dipped his hand in the water. Tasted it. It was sweet, beautiful and fragrant, as though it had been strained through deep moss. He drank a little and his heart lifted.

Jean now turned to the real question. He had been avoiding it through fear. Was his sister in this tomb? He had to know. For a second he hesitated, his stomach smarting with pain and hunger, his eyes drained for the moment of tears. Then with all his strength he pushed the lid of the tomb. He tried twice and each time fell back, his breath misting in the chill air. Then, as he was about to give up, something cracked in the stone. With his next push, the lid began to move. Slowly, it scraped aside, slowly. Now he was so close to its secret, he felt a familiar gripping terror. His mind, in a panic, cast back to the Library desk and the white, dust covered bones behind it.

Once the tomb was open, there was a disturbing smell of death and old air, but no last secret, no body, no *Papillon*.

Only water. It was a tomb full of clear water. It ran down the flute, dripped into the chamber and into the tomb. But why? It had been designed by the boys of the school. Bought by them.

Jean looked deeper. When the beautiful light hit the surface, he could see deep, deep, into the translucent calm. The water was clear and appeared to go on forever.

The water did not spill over the edge of the tomb. It must therefore go somewhere else. What had Moonster said? He must cross the Bridge to Dreams to see his sister. Was it here? No, it could not be that. He had seen the bridge. The bridge, a real bridge, was somewhere near the Head's room.

The more Jean stared at the water, the more he knew that the answer was in there. But he was terribly afraid of water. He always had been. Drowning was an awful way to die. Maybe even worse than starving in a tomb, if not nearly as bad as falling from a great height. But the sign said 'Aqua Est Vita', 'In water life'. What had he to lose?

With a shrug Jean slowly placed his face in the water and opened his eyes. He could see no further than before. He pulled his face out and shook his head like a dog.

There was not enough room for Jean to immerse himself totally. He went back to the loose flagging and dragged it to the centre of the room. This he used as a prop. With all his remaining strength he levered up the tomb lid.

Jean took a deep breath.

He took one last look around himself, carefully climbed up, and stood on the lip of the tomb. Then, he took a few deep, deep breaths and plunged headfirst into the icy water.

Jean swam down. What was the story this reminded

him of? The water babies; a nice story to read about the drowning chimney sweep, not so nice to live it. As he pushed himself downward, there was an underwater roaring and everything went black. A loud yet strangely muffled report reverberated in his ears. With a shock, he realised that the tomb lid had slipped into place again. Numb with cold, he swam upwards again. His head broke the surface and banged against the lid of the tomb. There was a little air here trapped in the small space between the surface water and the lid, but no escape. He bobbed around, growing ever colder, trying to shift the heavy tomb lid with his freezing hands. It would not budge.

Jean did not question it now. The questions and the reasoning were over. He had no choice. Somehow, he had kidded himself there was a choice.

Jean took some more deep, gasping breaths. His mind told him there was room to do a body flip but his heart was telling a different tale. He gulped air again and flipped over, immersing himself utterly. And then he went down, down into the black. As he descended, he pulled his hands against the sides for impetus. There had to be a way out, because otherwise the water in the tomb would simply have spilled out into the chamber. But did it just seep away through the ground?

And then Jean found what he wanted: a gap he could check. It appeared to be an underwater shelf. Was there another? No, only one. His lungs were almost bursting now. He pushed his feet off the wall and thrust into the corridor of water. It was a risk. If there was a wall before him, he would be knocked out. There was not. His body shot forward like a darting fish; his hands reaching before him. There was just enough room to do the breaststroke.

Jean's eyes hurt. His lungs were like a shut accordion desperate to be drawn. He was dying, dying. Everything in him wanted to give up, but he pushed on; another stroke and another. His hand reached for the ceiling. Was there air above his head? No. And now, as his mind began to fade, he saw the face of Mr Kay smiling and holding out his hand. Mr Kay was pointing to the blackboard, but there was no writing there, only endless pictures of the people he knew and had met, smiling and grinning and willing him to do something good with his life. He saw Moonster sitting in his high garret room grinning and holding his hands open to the skies. His Scottish mother as she covered her face to hide the tears from his dying father. Now he himself was about to die, but he saw the face of his father nodding and smiling from his hospital bed in Auxerre. What was he saying? Jean tried to see through the dimming light. And then he heard the whisper close in his bursting eardrums:

'Look after your sister.'

And Jean saw *Papillon's* face in all its beauty and innocence, her curling hair and laughing eyes.

'She needs you'

'And I need her,' Jean said in his dying head. He made one more stroke and thrust up his head. He opened his mouth and breathed in.

Icy air struck Jean's lungs. He thrashed around in the water, like a puppet whose strings have just been cut. There was air and space, a cavern of some sort suffused with dim light. Whatever it was, wherever he was, he was alive. Eventually, he managed to scrabble on to a small ledge. Jean slapped his wet arms around himself, noticing as he did so that, with the exception of some tatters, his paper armour had been shorn from his body by the icy water.

Jean shivered and shook in his dripping clothes, but his heart was bursting with warmth. He stood up, aware of a dim light that came from high above and the dim

227

flickering waters below him, and then he began to dance. He jumped up and down, leapt high and squatted and made a popping noise with his mouth. Jean was elated. He could have shouted but the popping noise was better. He had spent all this time being disappointed at not finding his sister and now he was elated that he had not found her. He jumped, he capered. She was not in the tomb. The tomb was an escape route like a Resistance tunnel or the Templars' hideaways in the small villages around Auxerre. Maybe it was Moonster's secret and he had not had the time to pass it on.

'Stuff that in yer craw!' he whispered, 'Mr Geography, I'm alive!'

The jumping and the popping had tired him out. Now, with his joy still burning low like a night light, he took stock.

The ledge was about a meter wide and stretched around in a curve. He could see a circular hole above him, tiny in the distance, which appeared to be the only source of light. There were movements in the air and sounds of water trickling nearby. Something dripped far away. Jean sensed he was a large place, like a cavern, but he could not be sure.

He could not see the far side of the ledge so he began to walk along it slowly, but first he made a cross on the ground with the wet chalk. He did this every two meters because at no point did the visibility improve. After about five minutes, he came to an opening shaft that apparently led to the outside. There was a grate over the front that looked as if it might be forced, with effort. He marked it in his mind and then began again chalking at intervals. He was nearly at the end of the chalk when he came to a second shaft but this one had no grate and he had to jump a gap. Here he saw his own chalk mark and he realised that he had made a circle.

A weight descended on him. He had been lucky once –

did he have to go under the water again? Maybe through the grille – but what if there was another grille or the way narrowed to a point and he got stuck?

The possibilities were endless, but mostly they ended in a nasty way. Was there nothing else he could do? He looked again at the ceiling, high in the distance. The light was tiny, like the morning star but it only cast a tiny reflection in the water. He scratched his head and as he did his hand struck something sharply.

Jean winced. 'Add that to the leg,' he thought and then reached up in curiosity. His fingers encountered what felt like a metal bar. Straight, horizontal, dripping with moisture. He felt around with both hands – there were two vertical bars on either side. What could they be for? He stood on tiptoes but could feel no further. He must examine what he could reach. Carefully, Jean explored the whole area. He ran his fingers over the cold, clammy surface of the horizontal bar. There appeared to be some writing etched into it. It took him a long time to work it out, but in the end there could be no mistake. The word there was: '*Papillon.*'

'Again!' Jean thought, fighting emotion. 'It must be a good sign. She's always been a good sign.' He sat and frowned, and then his own stupidity made him laugh. He turned and jumped upwards – caught the horizontal bar and reached higher to another, the twin of the first. It was a ladder! With difficulty, and scraping his knees, he drew himself upwards. Eventually, he was able to get a knee on a rung. After that, he was able to climb easily. At first he felt great about this, but then he thought again. His arms ached; he was tired; how high did he have to go? One look told him. Very high. And as he progressed, it became apparent that the ladder was old and in places broken or rusted. Once a section broke in his hands and he nearly cried out. It was a long time before Jean heard the broken metal strike the water. The noise was tiny and distant.

Jean had to take a rest. The ache in his right arm brought back memories of falling into the Head's classroom. It seemed so long ago. The memory awakened the hurt. His whole body seemed a mass of bruises and cuts. His stomach churned with hunger. He had to keep on climbing.

After a time, his world consisted entirely of blackness, the ladder and aching arms and legs. His knees and his head hurt and he felt hungry and dirty. Just when he thought it would never end, he realised that he could actually see better. The light was stronger. He craned his head back a long way slowly, as the rung on which his hands rested felt unstable. From this precarious angle, he could just glimpse the circle light above him. It emanated from a hole in the centre of the domed roof. The centre! How would he reach it?

As Jean contemplated this new problem, the ladder had suddenly come to an abrupt end, advertised by his hands finding empty space where rungs should be. He was stuck hundreds of meters from the ground with no way up and a long way down.

Above, in the wavering light he could vaguely discern the outlines of a door, but the ladder to it had crumbled away. There was also a rusted pipe below the door where water was partially trapped. Through this pipe, which apparently extended out along the inner circumference of the building, water flowed through a series of tubes and cylinders to drip-feed the pool hundreds of meters below. The whole construction, broken and jumbled up, pitted with rust, was disintegrating almost visibly before his eyes. Some of the broken spars extended towards the centre like the boughs of an old storm blasted tree.

Jean wept. He knew he had nearly made it. He knew that this was the way out. It had to be. And now to be so close.

For a full half-hour Jean clung to the ladder, at times banging his head on the steel wall. Then he stopped himself. What good was despair? Hadn't he proved himself resourceful in the recent past? He looked around.

It appeared from marks on the wall above that at some time some kind of platform had circled the whole structure, but it was ruined in part and inaccessible. Then Jean saw a letter in front of his eyes, in the place where he had been banging his head. It had been hidden by rust but the repeated impacts had uncovered it. It was the letter 'H'. What did it mean? For a full ten minutes, Jean scratched at the wall, uncovering more letters.

> **H>R> Y>O M>ST MAIE A IEAP >>>>**
> **IAITH INTO >>E C>>>TRE**

It was all Jean could read. He pondered on it for some time, and then he had it.

> **'HERE YOU MUST MAKE A LEAP OF ?**
> **INTO THE'** something?

At first he thought the last word must be 'core' and then maybe 'air' and then he saw that there must be space for three extra letters. It must mean 'centre'.

'Leap of faith,' he said aloud, shivering. His father had talked of a leap of faith. What did it mean? It was something to do with God, with belief. Logic could not help, reasoning could not help, Physics could not help. But was it a real leap? Did he have to literally jump or was it a symbolic jump? Soon, he reflected, he would have no choice. It would be a slip of faithlessness into nothingness. There would be a rush of air, the sound of a boy screaming and then it would be all over. Was not this what he had wanted anyway, when he had stood on the ledge at Park Grammar staring at the playground below? He could just let go of the ladder. His hands were cold and blue. His clothes were heavy and damp. Maybe it was time to lose them. Were they not just clothes around his soul? He could fall and within seconds he would not need clothes. His knees began to knock. His teeth were talking to each other. He was losing control of his body.

Slowly, Jean turned. It was difficult, but somehow he managed it. He clung, peering into the dim light, but could see nothing. Was there a blacker spot? His hands were going to slip. He began to utter noises; little whimpering things emerging from his head. Vibrations from his chilled feet knocked through his knees and legs, shaded his stomach, rattled his ribs and rolled around his head until they popped out of his mouth.

What if he could not jump? What if he did jump and there was nothing? Could it all be a trick by the Head?

'Nooooooo----h!' he screamed and pushed with all his force. As Jean sprang, his blazer caught on a rusty projection. Just a small thing, but it made his leap uneven. He tottered impossibly in the air.

There was a second when Jean's entire life raced across his eyes like a comic strip full of stereotypes, and then an incredible blow struck him in the chest. It felt as though his ribs had been stood on by an elephant. He bounced, his legs going forward and his arms going back. Some instinct made him grab with his hands and it was lucky that he did. He caught hold of something.

Jean hung in mid-air from he didn't know what. Afterwards, he had a chance to reflect that the thing was like the lip of a giant cup or the horn of a trumpet. But at the time he could only think of the terrible pain in his chest, the stopping of his heart, followed by a series of enormous palpitations. His thin weakened hands clung like a baby to the thing that prevented him from falling into nothingness.

Down there was likely death, and up was fear and uncertainty, but they were both better than *certain* death. Jean pulled himself upwards. He screamed, he cried, and slowly his body was drawn up. He let go with one hand, almost slipped, then managed to get one elbow over lip of whatever he held, and then the other.

It was incredibly difficult to get the rest of his body over, but somehow Jean did. He rested for a second on the edge of the thing and then he rolled over, faster and faster, until he dropped like a coin into a shaft and bounced out into the back seat of the strangest aeroplane he had ever seen.

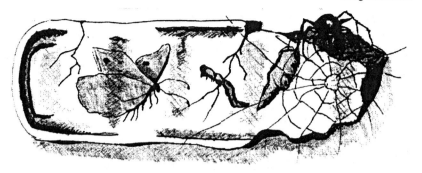

Chapter 24
The Paper Plane

All the other methods of escape had been attempted by somebody. This appeared much simpler to me--to stand on the roof and jump off.
- Bill Goldfinch

Long afterwards Jean was able to reconstruct roughly what had happened. The building he had climbed up was a disused water tower. Very near the top, in its centre, there was some kind of basin. This at some previous time had been fed water by the now rusted and broken pipes. Someone had diverted the huge central pipe to form a shaft that led into this separate but adjoining chamber.

The chamber was like a small aeroplane hanger and here was a contraption made entirely of paper. Or, as he looked closer, it appeared to be made of old jotters, news cuttings, writing; all schoolboys' writings, lines, punishments, timetables, exercises, maths problems. They were all jumbled, stuck, pasted and cut like a gargantuan origami into the shape of a bird.

And somehow Jean knew the bird was a white crow.

'Moonster's secret,' he whispered

'Yes,' said a familiar voice. 'Not many know of my secret. I knew *you* would find it.'

Jean looked upwards. Moonster sat in an open-fronted box, cross-legged, his back arched and his hands folded like a preying mantis. He was sitting in some kind of dumbwaiter that he had obviously transformed for his own purposes.

'You're building this aeroplane to escape?'

'Yes. I will escape. I have made room for others but the White Crow is mine alone.'

'Will it fly?' said Jean.

'It must,' Moonster replied. He slid down from the dumbwaiter on a heavy rope, looked briefly agitated, but regained his composure when his feet touched the floor. The two boys stared at each other for a space. Moonster shrugged. He rubbed his hands together. 'I waited for you as long as I could,' he said.

'Where?'

'On the Bridge to Dreams.'

'But I came through the graveyard, Geography.'

Moonster visibly paled. 'But how?'

Jean explained, Moonster all the while shaking his head. 'But that's amazing', he said when Jean stopped talking. He looked back at the shaft high up and the chute that projected from it like a child's slide. 'I explored it as best I could but it appeared to go just into nothing. And then the graveyard! I can only say you are very brave.' Moonster smiled and shook Jean's hand warmly. 'I am so proud to have known you.'

Jean felt a warm glow, despite his freezing clothes, and he embraced Moonster who laughingly said, 'But you are freezing. What can we do?'

'Have you a fire?'

Moonster laughed 'Here?' He pointed at the paper plane. They both laughed.

'But I can offer you a bun.' He pulled from his pocket an immaculately wrapped bun.

Jean could hardly quell his laughter. Eventually between laughs he managed to wolf it down. 'Well, I'll have to be wet a little longer, unless that other shaft leads somewhere warm.' He pointed to the opposing wall.

Moonster looked thoughtful. 'I don't know,' he said. 'Look over there.'

On the opposite wall there was another gaping shaft, the twin of the high shaft through which Jean had fallen. Clearly it had been attached to the high shaft but at some time in the distance past they had been separated or broken.

'Tell me the story again,' said Moonster thoughtfully.

Jean explained and Moonster stopped him at the part where he came to the 'Leap of Faith' message.

'Ah,' he said. 'That tower is full of writing. You were lucky to find the words to help you escape. Very lucky …or doomed'

'Grimshaw talked of a graffiti room?'

'No,' Moonster shook his head. 'I saw the graffiti room long ago.' His eyes glazed with the memory. He waited a space and then continued, 'The tower I have also seen from the top. Writing has a way of emerging in dark places.' He thought a little. 'Once this shaft might have led out – an escape route.'

'Or a trap.'

'Maybe,' said Moonster. 'I've only gone a short way down the lower chute. I hung on a rope. Couldn't risk any more. Many of the ladders are suspect, the avenues of escape or defence difficult. I've known Goobleys to frequent that area. You can hear them sometimes. You never know when they will appear.'

Jean recalled the flight through the attic rooftop. He

quailed inwardly.

Moonster continued. 'I've spent so long. So many years on the aeroplane. So many long years.' He raised his eyebrows and gave a wan smile. His single isolated canine tooth seemed more solitary because its companions were so uniform.

The entrance to the shaft looked menacing. The whistling of wind and mechanical knocking noises, subdued and far away, reverberated from the opening.

As they waited Jean said, 'Did you see my sister?'

'No,' said Moonster. 'Did you?'

'No,' replied Jean. 'Just as well. The tomb...' He gulped.

Moonster put a hand on Jean's shoulder 'It doesn't look good, I know, but this school is the strangest place and even here there is always hope.'

Jean nodded. 'Is this Hell?' he asked. 'Are we dead?'

'Maybe,' said Moonster. 'I often wonder myself. You see, it never appears to end. There are always lessons; there are always teachers, punishment, experiments. The boys come and they go, and it goes on and on and on. It is never a happy place.'

'How long have you been here?'

'I cannot remember.' Moonster looked at the aeroplane. 'But this wasn't built in a day.'

Jean nodded. The aeroplane was a vast testament to endless work. He could hardly imagine how Moonster had even transported the paper required to such an obscure location, never mind how he had glued it all together. He had then a vision of Moonster: all his plans, his strategies, his endless tasks and inventions, the secrecy of his life, the constant deceit, the hopes, the fears, the façade he maintained simply to exist. 'He must be very lonely,' Jean thought. But there was little Jean could do for him even if Moonster had wished it. They were both travelling different paths.

Jean pointed to the lower shaft. 'Is that another way out?'

'I come by the dumbwaiter.' said Moonster. 'This is an old water tower, but it backs on to one of the tallest parts of the school. If you take the dumbwaiter you can get into the water tower. The other direction leads to every level of the school in this wing.'

'Where does the dumbwaiter lead?'

'It passes floors and classes and ends in the Lost Cellars, so called since time began here, if ever it did. Maybe, it's because the cellars are lost, or those who go there are lost. I don't know. They form the limit of my exploration. Dark places. Goobleys everywhere, I expect.'

'Not the sewers then. I found your candles there when I first came in.'

Moonster frowned, recalling labyrinthine pathways in his mind. 'No. The old sewers run through the Lost Cellars, but I blocked the entrances off. It was not very pleasant and it took a long time.'

'I must go on looking for my sister.'

'Yes, I'll help you.'

'No, you have helped me enough. You carry on with your aeroplane, your White Crow.

Moonster smiled wanly. 'Will you try the shaft?' he asked after a space.

Jean looked at the opening, listened to the whirrings and clickings far below.

'No,' he said, 'I don't think I will.'

They walked to the dumbwaiter. Jean shimmied up the rope and crawled in. As he crunched up in the little box he said, 'Why is it called the Bridge to Dreams?'

'It's my name,' said Moonster. 'It's my dream. It crosses from the main buildings of the school to this tower and this aeroplane. So it is the Bridge to Dreams.'

'I hope for you it is not simply a dream,' said Jean. He

looked for the last time at Moonster's black trousers, maroon velvet waistcoat, watch chain and his absurdly spotted green bow tie. Jean smiled. Suddenly, Moonster grabbed the rope with one hand and pulled himself level to Jean. Their hands clasped. Moonster grinned back, showing his white teeth, one slightly askew, but there was a look of sad hope trembling like the wings of a tiny butterfly in his dark eyes.

Jean tried hard to fix every feature of his friend in his mind. Moonster's dim face so pale, so austere with his greased back, black hair: his small goblin ears and sharp chin. He took one long look and then Moonster finally shrugged as though some bizarre and private interview had ended.

'The Lost Cellars,' he said.

'Good luck,' they both said together.

Moonster had redesigned the dumbwaiter so that it could be operated by a pulley system on the inside. Moonster pointed to the left hand rope. He turned his thumb down and winked. Jean placed both hands on the rope and pulled. Slowly, the dumbwaiter descended. Moonster flipped over with the agility of an acrobat. The last Jean saw of Moonster was his upside down head and the single small wave of an elegant upside down hand.

At first there was only darkness but then suddenly a window would open out on a room. There would be a flash of colour and a tableau would enact itself for a second like a scene from a film or an illustration from a book. Jean's father had once related the tale of a bird that had flown from the dark night into a lighted banquet hall and then out through another window into the night. Jean felt this experience over an over again in the dumbwaiter. He felt like a man being reincarnated every two minutes.

Classes, lessons and innumerable pupils, all learning or unlearning something. And then Jean caught a

240

glimpse of the garden reflected in a mirror. The classroom was full but no one was looking towards the mirror. Their eyes were glued to the tall master who was slapping his hands on the tables, shouting loudly words that Jean could not catch. It sounded vaguely like the chant of a times-table, but there were words, ringing words, hypnotic and blindly obedient. Jean could still hear the words, like a phantom nursery rhyme, through a long period of darkness and then they faded away. Jean might even have fallen asleep. He never knew. All he felt was the jar of the dumbwaiter coming to a halt. All he heard was a low echoing thud, and he knew that he had landed on the bottom floor, the last rung of the school.

The Lost Cellars.

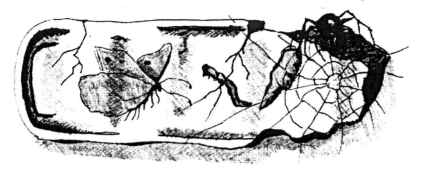

Chapter 25
The Lost Cellers

*In the cellars of the night, when the
mind starts moving around old
trunks of bad times, the pain of this
and the shame of that, the memory of
a small boldness is a hand to hold.*

- John Leonard

All around, it was quiet and still and infernally warm.
There was a still, heavy feel to the stifling air. Jean
could see nothing. He cursed himself for a fool.
Suddenly, he felt a shudder. The dumbwaiter tipped and
he was sent sprawling to the floor.

In the darkness, he heard the dumbwaiter moving,
going upwards again, no doubt. His hands scrabbled to
find it in the dark, but he was disorientated. Where was
it? If he jumped, would he be stuck half way and
snapped like a biscuit? And now there was only the
dark. How had the waiter tipped him out? Had
something pulled it? Jean got a sense that he was not
alone, just a feeling at the back of his neck, where the
hairs stood up like tiny regiments of soldiers. There was
something else here with him. Why did he not think to

243

bring a light?

Jean rose to his feet cautiously. At least he could stand up in this place. He raised his hands above his head: nothing. He stretched them out – and still found nothing. It was like being blind. He walked forward tentatively, feeling with his hands, and then retreated back a little way, bending closer to the floor. His hands struck something that made a little clinking noise. It was like a glass box; a lantern, he was sure. His hand reached further. He found several stubby sticks and after handling them a little decided they must be small candles. Jean thrust them into his pocket. Moonster would have left at least one. But where were the matches? Neither he nor Moonster had really thought this through.

Jean felt around himself again and suddenly his hand was gripping something warm and moist and wriggly. Something soft struck him. It was a hand in his and another flapping at him. There was a hiss and he kicked out. Goobleys! His feet touched something warm and there was the swift pad of rushing footsteps, scurrying away. Jean shouted. He heard his voice, still and small, rebound from the walls and beneath its echo the sense of other creatures, many of them, all around but backing away.

'What now?' Jean said to the darkness. The creatures began to creep back to him.

'Shouting is a reasonable form of defence, but it doesn't always work,' he thought.

And then he heard the creaking of the dumbwaiter, apparently descending once more. The sound, loud in the darkness, intensified. Slowly, behind Jean, a light surged like the beam of a lighthouse. A huge flare, flaming through the Goobleys. Jean could see them now in their multitudes, throwing up their arms to protect their huge misshapen eyes. They did not like the light.

Jean turned. Moonster had put a lantern into the dumbwaiter. He hoped his friend had not accidentally set light to his aeroplane before he had even attempted to fly it. Jean grabbed the lantern and whispered low *'Merci, mon copain.'* Beside it, there was a box of matches. Jean picked it up and with renewed confidence began to advance swiftly through the cellars, shouting 'Scat!' as he did so.

As he walked he bent down at intervals, chalking the floor with arrows. The light kept the Goobleys back, although Jean always felt their presence, as though they waited like demons in the penumbra beyond a salt circle.

Everywhere, in every room, along every corridor, in the high ceiling cupboards and in the recesses and alcoves, Jean looked for signs of his sister, but there was nothing of her to be found; only endless rooms and chambers that held old boxes and packing crates, rusting bicycles and projectors, filing cabinets, opened and locked, wooden chests muffled in musty straw, filled with beakers and old nets and footballs. All were immeasurably silent.

For the moment, the Goobleys appeared to have retreated beyond earshot.

In the silence, Jean began to come to terms with the futility of his search. He might be in these Lost Cellars for a thousand years before he came to their end. They might not even have an end in any real sense. He stalked through the cellars until his feet dragged and his stomach burned with hunger. His eyelids were like heavy weights. He had lost count of the candles that had guttered and failed, lost count of the times his weary hands had struggled to fight back the darkness with another tiny flame. The stub of his chalk had dwindled to a breadth of a fingernail. Now it was all nearly over. He wished for the hundredth time that he had let

Moonster help him but it was too late for regrets. He had tried and failed.

And then Jean heard a noise. Not the sneaky scurrying of the Goobleys, but a low throbbing like the sound of two great walls of a glacier grating against each other. For a long while, he sat on an old chest trying to identify the noise but he could not place it. He got up and walked a little further. Around him, rooms opened to other rooms and he could see rooms beyond them fading from the light of his lamp. Then the noise increased, only faintly but obviously getting louder. Jean saw, far in the distance, a red glow. Carefully, he picked his way over the rough floor. He listened for Goobleys, but now they seemed to have lost interest in him. In a strange way, it was disturbing that they had gone. He was reminded of the silence of a forest when the birds have fled, the empty instinctive dread of wild things afraid. Perhaps ahead there was something more frightening than the Goobleys themselves

As Jean drew close to the red glow, he took a chance and turned off the lamp. With the light gone, he was aware of a new and ugly smell. He shook his shoulders. Then he paced forward quickly, but on tiptoe.

The heat here was almost unbearable and Jean soon saw why.

In a large room, a huge fire was burning, so huge that Jean could have stepped into it with a whole cricket team. The flames leapt and licked upwards, sucked in by a giant chimney. The sight was so awesome that Jean's mouth dropped open and it was only after ten minutes of staring that he was able to see anything else in the room.

What he saw was a vast ceiling. It was criss-crossed with hanging ropes, nets and chains like a collapsing spider's web. Piercing through this entanglement, like a giant thumb, was a great chute about sixteen meters across; it spewed out rubbish, which was spilling into the room and piling up. Some of the rubbish looked ghastly in the light: prosthetic limbs, chairs, tables, paper, clowns' heads and circus animals: the conglomeration of a lunatic. Everything that you could think of, from anywhere you could think of, was spilling slowly into the room.

And then Jean saw the man. He was so small and unobtrusive that at first Jean had mistaken him for a piece of rubbish. The man held some sort of fork and he faced Jean, silently with an expressionless visage that seemed to burn in the light of the fire. He was clad in a grey overall that glowed pink in the light. On his feet he wore heavy black boots. 'NO boys allowed here!' he said in a sharp voice.

'Who are you?' replied Jean.

'I am the caretaker, the *janitor*.' The man lifted the fork a little and stroked it with one hand. 'No boys allowed. What are you doing here?'

'I'm lost and I'm looking for my sister.'

'You can't be both things at once.'

Jean decided not to argue. 'I'm looking for my sister.'

Suddenly, he felt a chill, even though the room was virtually a furnace and his wet clothes were steaming in the air. Behind the caretaker, he saw that what he had taken for stage props and prosthetic limbs were the real thing. They *were* limbs and not props. They were parts of people, heads and all. The awful smell came to life with a putrid intensity.

'What was her name?' asked the caretaker, moving a little closer.

Jean did not feel like saying anything. It had struck him that it was more like the time to throw up. But the caretaker's eyes were piercing him like twin blades in an Iron Lady.

'Her name was Michelle,' Jean said reluctantly. 'Some people here might have called her *Papillon*.'

The caretaker froze, even in the act of pacing forward. '*Papillon*. I know her name.'

'You know her?' In his eagerness, Jean forgot his horror and nausea and stepped forward, his eyes alight, burning brighter from inside his soul than the flames of the huge fire. 'Where is she?'

The caretaker grinned and his teeth blazed in the light of the furnace. He took the fork and with a stabbing harsh motion thrust it into a head that lay on the edge of the rubbish. With a swift expert motion he cast it, like a man pitching hay, into the furnace. He looked pointedly at the furnace and then he smiled a malevolent smile directed solely at Jean. He began to laugh.

The laugh was awful. It was human, but it had undertones of some animal in it, and was all the more awful because it came from something so clearly twisted. Jean looked away, unable to look upon the face of the caretaker. As he did so, he saw it.

Caught in the nets above the grotesque pile of objects, a pair of bedraggled yellow wings uncurled, as though a butterfly was gently dying in the heat of the fire. He felt a rush of anger and disbelief. 'You killed her?' he asked in a choking gasp.

'I am the caretaker of the school.' The eyes sparkled. 'Everything, everyone comes to me in the end.'

'Not me,' screamed Jean and he threw the lantern with all his power. It struck the small caretaker in the chest and he fell backwards. Jean did not even look. He ran into the glowing corridor as fast as his feet would take him.

The dull light from the room faded, as Jean ran further and further into the depths of the Lost Cellars. The endless rooms and chambers, passageways and halls reeled like a mad dance through black hell. He did not look behind to see if anything was following. He was not even afraid when the glow faded and he was left to walk swiftly, then slowly, to stand in the utter darkness of the cellar.

Jean stood for a few seconds, listening to the dying echoes of his last footsteps and then to the breathing in his head and the pounding of his blood. He began to calm down.

In the darkness, with the voice of his own body drowning the other sounds, noises began to creep in like little night animals around a dwindling campfire. The sounds of the Goobleys? Did it matter?

Jean felt utterly alone, betrayed by hope. He was terribly afraid. Not so much of the danger, but of the loneliness in his soul. He spat out in his disgust, choking on the acid bile in his stomach. He felt dirty and sick. His reason for being had been snuffed out. He could think of nothing but the black hole in the corner of his mind. The vast chasm of insanity and despair. There, in that empty corner, the abyss of darkness was growing and expanding. Its emptiness was becoming a tangible thing.

After a time, the external darkness began to weigh upon Jean like a dank velvet blanket. And then, from a source unknown, he felt the rising of a response to all the horror, all the fearful, sick images that rotated around in his brain like ghosts trapped on a Ferris wheel. They were nothing compared to the inner beauty he had found in a few odd places in this mad school. He would not give up! He would never give up.

Cautiously, Jean felt in his pocket for the little candles and breathed a sigh of relief when he found them - and the matches! He lit one of the candles.

He was standing in a corridor of some sort. There

were open doors on either side. One room appeared vaguely empty, the other seemed to be full of people. For a short while, he waited, listening, but there was no sound and nothing stirred. He walked into the crowded room.

There were old boxes and packing cases in a room full of stage props: helmets, swords, horses, globes, atlases. There were some figures near the far wall that Jean had mistaken for real men and women. Their silhouettes were outlined against an aluminium or silver-paper backdrop that reflected the light from the candle more intensely. When Jean drew up close, he saw that they were only mannequins in old period costumes blanketed in dust. In a corner, surrounded by sets of matte white paper armour, was a huge hulking carnival dragon, painted with the sigil of the worm Ouroborous, the great serpent of eternity that eats its own tale.

Jean sat on a packing case. He carefully placed the little candle on the rim of a Spartan helmet. The candle had only an inch or so left before it would gutter out, and then he had only one more candle and some matches. Maybe he could light a broken stick or something of the sort. He felt somehow that this would fail and there would only be darkness. The darkness would be like the darkness in his soul. It would never go away. But he would try to answer the darkness with something bright from within himself.

At that moment, in his mind's eye, he saw the haggard face of his dying father as he had last seen him in the hospital in Auxerre His father's life energy dipped and dimmed like the guttering candle. *'Papa,'* he mumbled quietly, 'please, please help me.'

As the image faded from Jean's mind, his weary gaze wandered to a battered shield lying on the floor.

He picked up a shield. There was writing on it in old crabby script. It said

There are seven forms of silence
The silence of an empty room
The silence of an empty heart
The silence in a graveyard
The silence in a tomb
The silence of two lovers
The silence between breaths
And the heartfelt silence

'Maybe,' thought Jean. 'But maybe not.' He thought of the writer trying, like himself, to get out of some kind of trap. Was this a sign from his father? The image had been so clear. Then suddenly he thought that his father might have died at that moment, and he had witnessed his spirit making one last appearance to help his son. As this miserable thought struck him, one of the Goobleys peered into the room. Jean saw the light shining from its loathsome eyes. He threw the shield at it in despair. There was a whimper and the sound of running feet and then, although he knew they were there, a space apparently cleared around him as though a witch had conjured up a pantacle.

No, it was something else. Jean looked at the huge carnival dragon in the corner of the room. What kind of hoard was it guarding? Was it a treasure trove?

The light flickered in the dragon's red eyes. Jean's movements had set its tongue wagging. It moved slowly like a leaf in a gentle wind.

'I wouldn't go in there,' came a low whisper.

Jean's heart missed a beat. But there was something familiar about the voice.

'Why not?' he asked, his gaze fleeting round the room.

'I can't move.'

And then Jean saw. It was the grey figure of Comedy,

hidden among the mannequins. His legs were crumpled beneath him, clearly broken. But he seemed not to notice.

'That's your last joke, I hope,' said Jean, not even caring how Comedy had come to this place or whether he suffered. Jean looked again at the dragon and then got to his feet with a growing resolve. 'I will not be beaten,' he whispered and tentatively he advanced towards it.

The dragon was a huge, terrifying beast. But Jean was afraid of nothing now. What else had he to lose? He reflected that he could light the shreds of his paper armour, if all other lights failed. With this resolution fresh in his mind, he drew closer to the dragon. It swayed gently, its old canvas and paper sides supported by a skeleton of bamboo. Jean opened up the huge jaws of the dragon and looked inside. Could he risk it?

He did.

Jean entered the dragon's mouth. He walked slowly through its body. He knew this was it. There was no place to run. Outside the Goobleys would see his shadow-form change colour as he moved along the plates of the dragon's vast scaled body. They would stand, like gruesome predators, observing campers in a thin-walled tent, waiting in anticipation.

The candle guttered. Jean's heart leapt. It was one thing to be resolved and brave, another to confront the moment. Suddenly, in the flickering stroboscopic moment, he saw at his feet the first steps of a spiral staircase. They led upwards. The dragon's body merged into these steps. The spiral stair formed its tail. How had Jean known this would be? Some inner instinct, something of the spirit, or help from beyond?

And then the candle flickered and died. Outside the dragon's body, he heard Comedy laughing in a slow, awful way.

There was a whooping noise, an ululation that grew

on all sides. Jean stamped his foot and shouted in response. His hands fumbled for and found the other candle but his scrabbling fingers could hardly hold the matchbox in his other hand.

In the body of the dragon, Jean was hopelessly trapped.

But he had seen the steps. He put one foot forward, but even as he did so a hand reached for him through the walls of the dragon and another punched him with a soft fist. He heard the crunching rip of paper as limbs and heads tore into the guts of the dragon. His own trembling hands thrust the matchbox back in his pocket. It was too late. The whooping rose around him, closer, fierce with ecstasy. The Goobleys had him. They were no longer frightened.

Jean began to run. In his head he had the steps visualised. They were like old castle tower steps, much like the Walter Scott monument in Edinburgh that he had visited once on a school trip with his Scottish mother. He could see her sad face in his mind's eye as he stumbled, fell and then half crawled, half ran.

Suddenly, there was a wrenching, ripping sound and Jean's body fell against something soft. He was fighting some huge billowing weight. He staggered back, shocked and baffled, his hands held out to protect his eyes.

There was light. Jean had found an open window. It had been shielded by an enormous velvet curtain, torn from its supports by his body. The window frame was bare and empty; its glass shattered long ago. Light poured over the empty casement like a cascading waterfall, utterly blinding him. He shielded his eyes with his hand and turned away. The Goobleys had stopped. He could sense them shuffling, waiting for him, but unwilling to risk the light.

Jean took a chance and, putting down the candle, he

jumped to the casement. As he did, the candle rolled downward step after step as though it had independently elected to desert him. There was no going back. He looked out. Below, a barren, concrete playground spread out like a grey blanket. There was a narrow ledge. Jean's eyes hurt. He could see buildings across the paved ground, but they appeared oddly unfamiliar, given his recent experiences.

Jean pulled himself a little along the ledge. He came to a window festooned with old musty ivy. An ancient classroom reposed in silence. It was dimly lit and through the lattice of ivy he could see that it was empty of people.

For some reason, Jean felt terrified of the empty room. His eyes, still almost blind, did not recognise its features, but his heart knew exactly which classroom it was. For a second longer he stared, until his gaze travelled up the tiers of sepia desks and fell upon the vague blur of a large, familiar picture framed above the old school desk. He battled with his imagination. The picture appeared empty, the Head either removed or hidden by some trick of the light. Did the bleak landscape of sad gravestones stretch out in weary silence, eerie and lonely? Or was there still a horrific shadow there, waiting? Jean's mind was weaving like a drunk. His smarting eyes could simply not discern whether the Head was in the picture or not and that inspired the awful thought that somehow he might be in the classroom itself.

There was a sudden flash of distorted light. It was as though he stared through a broken kaleidoscope to a distant, impossible galaxy. The door opened in the classroom, and such was his fear that Jean almost fell back in his efforts to get away from the window. Even as he did so, he caught a brief glimpse of a small girl, clad in a blue skirt, her eyes staring at him in admiration.

Jean would never be sure if it was *Papillon*. It seemed so like her, but the light, the distance and the distortion might have made him imagine what he merely hoped to see. There was simply no time to tell.

Impelled by his fear, Jean lurched helplessly along the tiny ledge. He careered like a gyroscope teetering on the brink of inertia. Wild images strained to break from his brain. His body tottered and twisted. And then, before he could help himself, he slipped and started to fall. His mind pulled him back to the classroom. His body still moved under its own volition. He grabbed a guttering, pulled, spun and then fell.

Through a window.

He landed with a crash upon the floor.

Jean hit his head, but it did not knock him out. It was painful though and he sat holding it in agony, while around him rose a terrible crashing like the amplified march of a battalion. There was a rending tear and the door beside him broke in.

Jean's hands scrabbled for a weapon but there was nothing in his pocket save a tiny fingernail of chalk and a key. He could see no way out.

'Goobleys,' he said.

But it was the school caretaker, dressed in his grey overalls, holding a massive jemmy in one small fist.

Behind him stood Mister Kay, behind him the vague blur of his Head of Year, Miss Kennedy, and all around were the familiar surroundings of the Geography stockroom at Park Grammar. Through the frame of the broken door, Jean could see a classroom so familiar it seemed almost absurd.

The adults stared in astonishment at him. At first their faces were angry and then the expression on Mr Kay's face changed to concern. He pushed past the caretaker and knelt down. 'Are you okay, Jean?'

'Yes,' said Jean. 'What happened to my sister?'

Mr Kay opened his mouth to speak and then his eyes appeared to film over. 'We'll get you to the nurse,' he said hesitantly. 'We can answer questions later.'

'Mr Kay,' said Jean, 'I need to know now.'

Mr Kay sucked in his breath. He looked carefully at Jean. And then with a strange and bizarre curiosity, his hand reached out to Jean's neck as though he was about to caress him. 'That's your sister's locket. She was wearing it this morning before...' His shoulders appeared to slump a little. He swallowed.

'Before what?' said Jean and his own hands reached to the locket.

'She didn't come back to school after lunch. She's missing,' Mr Kay said finally.

'I know,' said Jean.

Mr Kay nodded his head.

Jean reached up and clasped his hand firmly. 'But I'll find her.'

The adults parted, allowing Jean a gap to walk through into the classroom. They stared at him in silence, as he stood in the centre of the room dripping in his musty, bedraggled uniform. He examined the rows of clean desks, the polished floors and the murals of distant lands decorating the classroom walls.

Without looking back, Jean walked out of the open door.

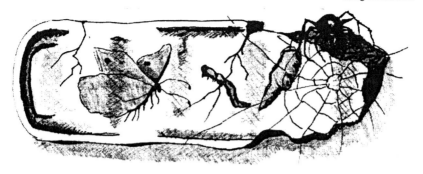

Chapter 26

Omnium   rerum   principia   parva sunt.

- Cicero

Jean lay on the ground of the back porch. He guessed that he was as cold as the spaces between the stars wheeling above him. 'It's quiet,' he thought.

In the moonlight shadows Jean could only just discern the cocoon of the caterpillar, still there under the leaf like a seed about to burst. *Do caterpillars feel the cold?* Even his brain was freezing. *Do they hear anything in there? Do they sleep, do they dream?* There were too many questions. His body seemed to be disappearing. When it had gone there would only be questions.

Now, for the first time, Jean saw the spider. How he could not explain, but he knew that it had been there all the time. It waited above the cocoon, the silver strands of its web caught in the star light. The web spread like a fisherman's net trawling the air above the cocoon. When the butterfly emerged, it would have to be very lucky to escape the web.

The moon was full, its pitted surface like the battered shield he had found in the Lost Cellars. The words of the unknown poet were etched on his memory: 'There are seven forms of silence. One is the silence of an empty heart.' Jean felt that silence like a palpable thing. 'Is there more silence out there?' He thought. 'Does it add up like numbers: silence plus silence equals more silence?'

Jean stared at the cocoon. By the illusion of perspective the cocoon already seemed to be caught in the web. But a million miles beyond, through the strands of the web a single star glinted like the head of a pin.

'It begins with hope,' thought Jean. 'You see the light. You don't see the web.'

In the morning the butterfly would emerge. The spider would be waiting in silence.

So would Jean.

Printed in the United Kingdom
by Lightning Source UK Ltd.
125091UK00001B/120/A